WILLOW OAKES

Jennifer

Luing

Schafer

Willow Oakes

DEDICATION

First, I want to thank God. Without God this would not be possible. I want to thank my friends and family for their unconditional support. I am not sure what I would do if it weren't for your never-ending love and support so I can live my dream. Jeri Ann my editor; thank you for your hard work and patience to make this come to realization, Peighton and Stacy Henningsen for the brilliant artwork, and finally you the reader for purchasing my book. You are the reason I do what I do. I hope you enjoy meeting Willow and her friends. I hope you continue with us on her developing journey.

PART 1

CHAPTER 1

It was a cold, fall day. You could feel the weather changing in your bones. Willow knew way before the winds came in, the weather was going to change. More the just the weather, the wind was going to bring in other changes too.

In some cases, change is good. For example, spring is a chance for one to make new dreams and goals for themselves. But she was not sure everyone was ready for the change in this fall season. But like the coming winds, she could not do anything to stop the change from happening.

Someone was burning wood, hickory to be exact. Willow sat in the chair on her porch and took the sights, sounds and smells all in. She looked at the plant beside her and noticed a web on the leaves that a friendly spider had woven during the light of the moon the previous night. The spider itself was as big as a coin. The turquoise blue marking on its back was in a shape of a perfect triangle. She looked at the spider's masterpiece of the web and realized it was very beautiful. The web was totally unscarred. She knew that would not be the case in an hour. Some poor bug would fall into the spider's trap and be its meal. The bug would face the cruelty of the hungry spider. As soon as the thought entered her mind, a cobalt blue butterfly fluttering by almost landed on the web. She put her hand out to rescue the beautiful butterfly from an almost certain death.

"I don't know which is more beautiful—the butterfly or the person it is perched upon," a voice said, bringing her out of her trance.

"Hello, Adam."

"Hello. I didn't see you at the market today."

"I was not feeling well so I stayed home. There is much to do when you live alone."

"I bought you some herbs. I saw them and thought of you. The lady who sold them to me said they were good for healing. I am sure you know that though."

"Thank you. I appreciate your thoughtfulness. How much do I owe you?"

"Nothing. It is gift."

"Adam, you know it is not proper for a woman to accept a gift from a man, especially a single woman."

"I won't tell anyone if you don't."

"I need to give you something."

"Hmmm. Do you have any of your strawberry pie?"

"Yes, I do. Just one moment and I will get you a slice." She replied and left to get them both a piece of the fresh pie.

Willow let out a breath when she entered the house. She didn't realize she had been holding her breath from the moment she knew Adam was in her presence. She didn't know what it was about him that made her hold her breath.
Adam was different than the other men in the village. His blue eyes seemed to reflect his kindness. He didn't think her herbs were odd. Or the many other items she used when others in the community thought they were peculiar.

Willow realized she was leaving him out there all alone. She knew if she was not out there fast, the rumor mill would be busier than the spinning wheel. While she was quickly cutting two pieces of from the pie, she carelessly cut her hand in the process.

"Oh my!" She exclaimed, as she reached for a towel to cover her hand to h
elp stop the bleeding. A stream of crimson blood escaped the towel and started to travel down her arm. She quickly wrapped her hand and carried the delicious-looking pie out to the porch.

"What happened?" Adam inquired.

"I am a clumsy woman. I sliced my hand along with the pie."

"Are you okay?" He asked anxiously as he took her hand.

"Oh, it's just a minor cut. I will put some ointment on it and keep it wrapped. I will be fine. Eat your pie." She answered nonchalantly.

"Let me wrap it better for you."

"Adam, I am fine. It is not an angry cut. The only thing that will be angry is me and your stomach if you don't eat." She replied jokingly.

He took a bite and the smile on his face said it all. He liked her pie. He liked her company. They sat on the porch and made small talk about the weather.

Willow liked to see him smile. There was a certain dance his eyes did when he smiled. She loved talking with Adam. There was a part of him that held a certain sadness. She couldn't quite put her finger on it just yet; but she knew she would in time. A lot of things came to her in time.

"Thank you again for the herbs. It was nice of you to think of me."

"Thank you for the pie."

"You are more than welcome. Tomorrow I am picking gooseberries."

"Wonderful"

"You should go now. There is sure to be talk if you stay much longer."

"Let them talk. Small minds lead to big mouths."

"I don't want to ruin your good name."

"What about your name? I don't want to ruin yours."

"My name was ruined before my first breath was taken into my body."

"That's not how I see it. But it is getting late and I will go. Not because I am afraid of tarnishing my reputation; but I think too much of you to tarnish yours." He said as he gave her a smile and got on his horse.

Willow watched Adam ride off a little bit before going inside. She reached in her pocket and retrieved the satchel of herbs he had brought her. She put the pouch to her nose and knew immediately what the herbs were for--cuts and scrapes. How did he know she would cut her hand? Willow was completely out of the herbs she usually had to cure such cuts. She knew the cut would turn angry if she didn't put something on it. She had been prepared for one angry cut. But now she didn't have to worry, thanks to Adam.

Willow went immediately to work making a salve to calm the cut made by the carelessness of a giddy woman with a knife. She smiled as she unwrapped the bloody towel her hand. She should have known better to have paid her full attention and respect to the knife as she was cutting the pie.

She carefully took the white makeshift bandage off of her hand. She could see crimson on the white cloth like an irritated wasp when you torment its nest. The wound had already produced an angry scarlet scab with pink surrounding the scab like a circle around the sun on a hot day. The salve will help calm the anger of the scab. Quickly Willow mixed the ingredients together and placed the salve on her wound. She let out a little cry of pain from the stinging the salve made. The wound shed a few tears in the form of yellow liquid before calming down. Then the salve felt cool and calming against the sore. She found a new white cloth and wrapped her hand once more as the salve sunk into the wound to heal it. In the morning, the wound would show its emotion on the hand. It could be an angry red like a spoiled child not getting his way or a cool pink like a child waiting patiently for his desires. Willow hoped it was the latter.

CHAPTER 2

Willow could hear the skies begin to let loose with much needed rain. She hoped Adam made it home in time. The thought of him brought a smile to her face.

She started to reminisce about the day she first saw him. It was fall at the Marketplace many years ago. It was much like a day like this one that was coming to an end. Willow was trying to get a large, delicious-looking, shiny apple from the over-loaded apple tree. The apple she wanted was just beyond her reach. She jumped as high as she could several times but without success. She stopped and stared at the apple as if she was going to burn a hole into the center of it. She stared and counted to three to calm herself. When she reached the number three, the apple graciously fell to the ground without bruising the fruit. She was happy. She was surprised. The apple just conveniently fell to the ground. She was sure it was luck. She had nothing to do with the falling fruit. She was a child! She just wanted to eat the apple because she was hungry.

When Willow finished her snack, she returned to the Marketplace. She and her mother sold liquids, herbs, teas, and salves among other things at their stand at the market. Her mother let her wander to experience other specialties people had to offer the world. Her mother said one shouldn't be so closed-minded that a little bit of sun cannot enter in.

Willow remembered a beautiful lady dressed in the bluest dress the young girl had ever seen. She thought that blue dress put the bluest sky to shame. That day the beautiful woman came up to the stall where her mother and she had their items and smiled.

"Good day Madam, how can we be of service to you today?" her mother asked politely.

"Good day. I have heard many good things about you and your plants and liquids."

"I hope all is good. I know many who don't believe."

"I don't put much stock in the talk of fools. I need your help. I was looking at my flowers when a thorn wedged itself into my hand and has become very angry. I was wondering if you have a salve that may calm it down."

"Here is a small amount of what I have," Willow's mother said as she handed her a little of some salve. "Come by my home tomorrow and I will make you a full dose."

"Thank you so much," she smiled before a young man came up to her.

"Mother, Father wanted me to come and gather you so you can look at something," a young man of about eleven said.

"Of course," she said to the boy. Then turning her attention back to the mother and Willow, she continued, "Thank you for your time. I will see you again soon." She then turned to leave.

The woman and her son had been gone from the stall only but a few of moments when the young Willow noticed the woman had left her salve on the table.

"Mother, she left her ointment," she exclaimed.

"Here, child. Go and give this to the Madam. Tell her she left her mirror at the table. You must be discrete for her husband must not know this came from us. If he finds out, he will be angrier than the thorn in her hand," Mother commented before placing a silver container in her hand.

The young girl walked as fast as she could to find the woman and her son. Willow tried to yell at her and get attention but the crowd but the horses made it impossible to for the woman to hear. She decided to run before the beautiful woman got into her carriage and drove off.
Willow did not see the trotting horses until it was too late. She thought there were seven of them. She was sure she would be trampled and this would surely be her fate. She closed her eyes to help prepare for the impact when she felt herself falling, her shoulder crashing into the ground. Willow opened her eyes slowly, not prepared to see her fate. What she saw instead was the face of the woman's son.

He didn't say a single word to her. He just smiled like an angel. He extended her hand and helped her up. The two youngsters didn't say a word to one another. They both knew what the other one was thinking. Neither one of the youngsters knew that this was the last time they would see one another for eight years.

CHAPTER 3

Willow found herself smiling as she remembered her mother. She missed her so at times her body ached. She was close to her mother. Her mother taught her everything she knew and continued to teach her every day. Mother's body may be in the ground but she was not forgotten.

Willow looked up at the heavens, closed her eyes, said a few words to herself as spun around with her arms wide open. She circled three times before rain came down. At first, it came in little droplets. Then, all at once, the rain came down heavily, soaking her and everything around her. She laughed and danced in the rain until her clothes stuck to her slender body.

The cool water felt good on her skin. She could feel the hard ground melting under her feet into a warm glorious mud. The skies began to talk to her with their thundering voices followed by their electrifying cries. The wind joined in to add a bit of variety to the situation.   She danced her way to the covered front porch, sat down in her wooden rocking chair and watched the wonderful show Mother Nature provided.

She looked over to the west.   The clouds were dark as the night that was fast approaching. Willow didn't mind the night. At times, she preferred it to the day. Daytime provided the warmth of sunshine. She loved to feel the heat on her face. The warmth of the sun reminded her that everyone and everything has good in them. But they also have a spirit that if provoked can harm.

The nighttime was different. The night leant to renewal. A time of letting go of the day and getting ready to start anew. The moonlight on her skin gave her peace, energy and solace. Mother Nature sang a different song at night. Willow felt you could be your true self at night. You could tell much about a person by how they looked in the moonlight. A wise person once told her a person's soul shines bright in the moonlight. Secrets seems to appear in the moonlight if you look hard enough for them.

Along with the gentle rhythm sound of her rocking, she could hear the sounds of the crickets singing their song. The frogs in Bethany Pond soon joined in. Lastly, the nocturnal bats added to nature's symphony. The full moon finally emerged out of the thin blanket of clouds.

Willow looked beside her and could now see the web beside her more clearly. The spider was back at work again, adding to her exquisite masterpiece. However, Willow's masterpiece would take an enormous amount of patience and time. Every single step had to be perfectly orchestrated to make sure the final product was as magnificent as the creator and the observer. Unlike the friendly spider who knew the purpose of her masterpiece, Willow did not have any idea where, or when, she would need her masterpiece. All she knew in her heart was that patience was essential in this task. The time and reason would be revealed when the moment was right.

CHAPTER 4

Willow grabbed a handful of dried herbs and threw them into the fire. The fragrant plants crackled and displayed variations of vibrant oranges and reds. She smiled as she stared at the color show. The colors reminded her of autumn. She loved all the seasons but fall kept a special place in her heart. The changing of the dressings on the trees was a wondrous sight to see.

"With these leaves into the fire. Only you know what will transpire. Keep thee safe from harm's way and reveal the truth on the right day." Willow spoke the words as she stared intently into the glowing blaze. The flames transformed from reddish-orange spikes to ones dancing in a circle as if they were joined hand and hand. She looked out the window and saw the shining moon hidden behind a few trees in the yard. Willow yawned and finally realized she was tired.   She undressed and laid down on her soft bed.

Her thoughts reviewed her day and she smiled. She met two new friends today, the spider and the butterfly, and she saw Adam. It rained. And the moon and stars tonight were the best artwork of the night sky. As she closed her eyes, she fell asleep in a matter of moments with a peaceful mind and a hopeful heart.

Willow's dreaming mind again brought forward the first time she met Adam. However, the recollection wasn't about him, but of his mother. Her mind replayed that first meeting as if it were happening for the very first time. Only this time, the details were sharper. The colors were more vibrant. The smells of the Marketplace tickled her nose.   She could also hear the vibrant sounds of the Marketplace. It was noisier than she remembered. She was taking it all in a new way. And, in this memory, she was not eight but her current age.

Adam's mother stood out in the Marketplace. She was the most beautiful woman in attendance. Her blond hair sparkled with shimmers of gold, like honey when the sun hit the strands just right. Her flawless skin matched her honey-colored hair with the right amount of pink that made her face glow. Her voice was low, soft, and kind. Her smile was as bright as the sun. It provided a welcoming feeling to whomever was around. She was the type of person you were naturally drawn to.   You wanted to be in her presence. Even in her village dress, she was the best-dressed woman in the Marketplace. She was trying to fit in by not flaunting her circumstance. Even though she tried well, one could almost tell she was not from the village, but most people knew her standing.

Willow noticed something about the mother's dress. There was something odd about the garment. That mesmerizing dress, if positioned in a certain way, almost blinded anyone who was directly looking at it. Mr. Wells, who was standing about six feet from the woman, was extremely bothered by the vision. Willow and her mother, who standing next to him, were not affected by the dress at all. Mr. Wells became so annoyed by the feeling, he moved away in disgust.

Willow's mind followed Mr. Wells to the tavern. A group of men were at a table in the old smelly tavern. It smelled of yeasty beer, old-boot feet, and other musty odors that seemed to constantly remind the occupants of the tavern to take a good bath early this month. One red-faced man, whom she did not recognize, was shouting and pounding his fists on the table, making the spirits in the pewter cups do a dance.

The other men were shouting out their thoughts and feelings too. Willow could not decipher what they were trying to say. She tried to focus her hearing to listen clearly to the men's words; but she didn't succeed. The man's hard pounding was the only thing she could hear. The sound crescendoed so much, she had to close her eyes to drown the clatter out to concentrate. One last big pound on the table and her eyes came open with a hard start matching the pounding of the table. She realized it was just a dream and the banging was coming from her own front door.

Willow glanced out her window. The moon was still high in the sky with the stars dancing in its light. It was quite late. Who could be up at this hour? Why were they pounding at her door with such force and urgency? She put on her robe, grabbed her candle, and went to her door.

"Who comes to my door at this hour?"

"Pardon the hour, Madam. It is Timothy Bart."

"Mr. Bart. How can I help you? Come in, please," she said as she opened the door to a flushed-faced man.

"Thank you. Again, I apologize for the lateness of the hour. It's my Anna. She has not quit crying for three hours."

"Oh, the trials of new fatherhood." She murmured as she put on the kettle and lit more candles.

"Oh, if it were only that simple!"

"Take a seat, take a breath, take a sip and tell me all about it." She encouraged as she set a cup of steaming liquid in front of him.

"But I must get back! Her mother is exhausted to the point of tears!" he exclaimed, the urgency coming back to his voice.

"Timothy, I promise your girls will be okay. You must care for yourself also. You have time for a small cup of tea, a rest, and a breath," she encouraged him as she sat down to drink her own tea.

"Thank you." He replied with a weak smile.

"Tell me, Timothy, how are your girls?"

"Anna is growing like a weed. She is a true blessing. Sarah is a good mother. She dotes on the child, as do I. The good Lord has blessed us and with the rain He has blessed us all." Timothy smiled, becoming more relaxed.

"Good to hear. Children are a true blessing; not just to their parents but to all who love them. True love is priceless. The Good Lord knows what we need before we know."

"But He who giveth, can take away."

"You speak words of truth. How's your stomach?"

"How did you know I was under the weather too? I mentioned nothing of the sort," he asked in surprise.

"It's not a hard puzzle to figure out. New father, crying baby, a husband who feels helpless. Then if you add no rain for weeks. All those worries add to wrinkles, a few gray hairs, and aches," she joked with her visitor.

"Well, no wrinkles or gray hairs plague me yet. I do feel better. The storm in my stomach has subsided, thank you."

"Take this pouch of tea. Warm it in a cup of water. You and Sarah drink it. Have Baby Anna suck on the pouch the next time her stomach is hard. You all shall sleep well and feel better when you wake," she instructed as she handed him a black woven pouch.

"Thank you so much! Thank you for the tea, advice, and pardon again for the hour."

"No need for apologies. Now go home to your girls. Sarah is fretting that she is failing as a mother and a wife. She needs a hug. Hold her tight, Timothy. She loves you so much and wants to make you happy. Safe travels," Willow said as she opened the door for him, watched him get on his horse and ride away.

She could hear an owl hoot in approval of her actions. Willow looked down at her friend's masterpiece. The spider was still working her magic, only stopping for a brief moment as if she were seeking approval from the woman.

"Keep going, my darling. You will do great things," she said aloud to the spider and to herself.

Willow could tell by the conversations of the night creatures that it would be a few hours before the sun was fully awake. She was tired and needed to rest her mind, eyes and body. She went into her house, checked the embers in her fireplace, blew out her candles and went back to bed.

Rest would not come to her as easily this time around. She and the covers did a tango to the music of the night creatures. Her mind would not stop long enough for her to take in the dream. Rapid flashes of images came into her mind. She tried to slow them down, to see what her mind was trying to convey to her. But she could not slow it down. The flashes were like thunder and lightning during a storm. She didn't know where this dream was taking her, but she knew it was a journey of peace. She finally drifted off to sleep.

CHAPTER 5

Willow felt a warmth of heat upon her face. The sun woke her from her deep slumber. She woke up to quite a different symphony than the one she fell asleep to the night before.   The birds were alive with vibrant chirping, instantly making her heart smile like a child on Christmas morn.   The frogs, not to be forgotten or ignored, bellowed out their baritone sounds. But those low sounds were as sour as the gooseberries she needed to pick for the day's pie and jellies. She loved each of the beautiful symphonies equally. There was beauty in each of the harmonious melodies.

She picked out a perfect frock for the coolness of the morning. It was one of her favorites--a plaid pattern of red, orange and yellow. The pattern had the colors her of her favorite season, autumn. She knew the morning air would be chilly so she grabbed her wrap of the same colors. She put a kettle on the stove and prepared to start her day. The kettle finally screamed good morning and she made a cup of tea. She went to sit in the rocking chair on the porch to enjoy the music of the morning. When she stepped out the door to greet her day, her eyes traveled to the masterpiece of her friend. The web was like a piece of lace she had seen for sale at the Marketplace. The web was delicate and strong. It was like the creator. The spider's friend, the butterfly, landed nearby to keep her friend company.

Willow sat down and took a deep drink of her hot, steaming liquid. It warmed her body and brought a smile to her face. She really loved her little cottage. Her home set high on a hill about half a mile from the village. It was close enough where she could hear the bustle of the city, but quiet enough where no one bothered her. Everyone knew where she lived but she did not receive many visitors. Near one edge of the village was a forest. At the forest's edge was Adam's house. If you walked long enough through the forest, it gave way to the most beautiful meadow.

She was not blessed with riches, but Willow was blessed with nature all around her. To her, she was the richest person in the village. She could see glimmers of lights flickering like fireflies in the early hours of morning. Willow could hear the moaning of Mr. Ballerton's cattle greeting whomever was awake and listening. Widow June's rooster was not going to be outdone. His vocal alarm rang so loud it would have woken her, if she was not already awake.

Willow loved her simple life. She wanted for no material things, for those things break or fall apart. They would eventually diminish into nothing but scraps. She longed for companionship. She was happy with her own company, but someone to talk to about her day would be wonderful. She didn't have many people she would deem as a true friend she could talk to. Sure, there were people in the village who came knocking like Timothy. But no one comes knocking at her door just for the sake of checking on her well-being. The thought made her sad, but only for a moment. If she learned anything in her life, it was that life is too short to be sad or regretful. She needed to live the life God gave her. Just like Timothy said, "God giveth, God taketh away." God had taken a lot away in the last ten years, but it only made her stronger.

Willow could see the sun rising above the hills towards the trees. The forest is where her day would begin. The thought of going to the forest excited her. Many people steered clear of that area. She didn't understand why. Silly superstitions were her guess. People avoid what they fear.

She couldn't hold her excitement any longer. She finished her drink. grabbed her shawl and basket and trotted down her driveway to the path of the forest. She was headed to one of her favorite spots in the world.

The journey to the forest was not a hard nor long one. The blue sky, the beautiful sun beams, and the soaring birds provided the perfect scenery. She hummed a tune. She could not recall where she heard it nor the origin of the melody. But the melody came to her as easily as breathing.

Willow kept scanning the sights and walking as if she were exploring the journey for the first time. In reality, this was one of many. No matter how many times she came to the forest, or will come to the forest, there is always something new to discover. Nothing in life ever stays the same forever. Life continues no matter what is going on with your own. Even the sun shines differently than it did the day before. The birds add or take away a few notes from the song they sang the hour before.

As she traveled deeper into the forest, she sensed she was not alone in her own company. The sensation of another person didn't alarm her. Whatever or whomever had joined her was not out to harm her. They were just curious of what she was doing. Willow said nothing, just went on about her business. She was not going to acknowledge her mysterious companion, for he or she would make his or her presence known at the appropriate time.

Willow could smell the scent of the ripe gooseberries, thanks to the subtle westerly wind breezes. She went to the bush, picked a few and took a bite of one. The sourness of the fruit bombarded her mouth in an instant, making her eyes water due to the bitterness of the berry. She smiled as she picked one after another. Such a tiny fruit that packed such an impactful reaction, like a mustard seed. She picked the berries for a little more than half an hour, having gathered three-quarters of a basket. She was still humming her song with the accompaniment of nature's creatures. All was going well until she heard a crack of a twig interrupting her song along with her thoughts.

"Hello? Who's there?" She called out.

There was no answer.

"Please make your presence known!" She called out again into the open.

The feeling of being watched totally vanished. She went back to her picking. She almost had an entire basket of the ripe fruit. The whole basket would make two good-sized pies or even a large-sized cobbler. She suddenly realized she was hot and thirsty. She decided to sit under a tree to cool herself. The canopy of branches and leaves made a perfect shade from the sun. The wind was picking up and the breeze felt good. She was still warm, so she undid a couple buttons from the top of her dress to allow the air to reach her bosom. The cool breeze was quite a welcomed relief. She took off her shoes to wiggle her toes in the breeze. She laid her head back on the rough bark of the tree and closed her eyes. She breathed a sigh of relaxation and listened to the lullaby of the forest before drifting off to sleep.

The argument between thunder and lightning and the crying of the clouds brought her awake with a start. Willow forgot where she was for a brief second, turning her head and standing up with a start. She forgot about the basket of gooseberries in her lap. The basket fell to the ground and gooseberries scattered out of the basket onto the forest floor. She heaved a sigh of disgust, only to feel better knowing the food would be a good meal for the animals.

The raindrops were getting bigger and the argument was getting louder and more intense moment by moment.   The winds started to blow a little harder now, letting the forest know change was on its way and you would be wise to not fight with her.

She looked around the forest. She could see the animals scampering for shelter. She knew she herself needed to seek shelter herself. The village was too far away for her to run to at the moment. And her home was even further. She knew if she tried, she would be putting herself in grave danger.

Willow heard an owl land on the ground, grab a berry, and start to hop on the ground.   The owl would take a couple of hops and then look back at her. She picked up a couple of berries and threw them to the owl who rushed to get them. The owl then looked up at the sky, to Willow, and then the forest.

"Do you want me to follow you, dear one?" she asked the bird.

The feathered bird hopped to her feet. The owl grabbed another berry then trotted into the forest stopping to make sure Willow was following. The owl had a calmness about it. The storm did not seem to bother the wise bird in the least.   Thunder clapped so loud it seemed to shake the ground making the situation to find shelter critical.

"We must not waste time, or we both will be soaked to the bone. Lead the way, dear friend." Willow said as she reached down to touch her new friend. The bird was not scared of her. The owl nuzzled Willow as if they had been friends for a long time. The bird went from a trot on the ground to flight in the air. Willow started walking at a steady pace then eventually her walk turned into a run. She lost track of her flying friend. The rain started to come down heavily, now blinding her vision.

Willow knew this forest well and she knew there was no shelter in the direction she was traveling. She should have turned the other way and went back to her house. It was too late now. She was in the middle of the forest and she had to trust her new friend. In the air, the owl had a better view of the forest.

Willow was about ready to give up when she heard the cry of her new friend. She knew she had to follow the cry. Thankful for the warm weather of the day, she knew she would not become ill from being so wet. The heat of the day, when it returned, would dry her in no time. She stopped for only a second when she heard the cry again. She had to keep going. She turned toward the cry when she saw the owl on the ground by a hill.

"You brought me to a hill? Dear one, I cannot dig," Willow chided as she bent down to pet her guide.

The bird started to peck the hill. She watched the bird to see what was causing the odd behavior. Was she being silly following a bird? Was the bird struck by lightning and was not quite right? She was about ready to turn and head for her home when the sound of the pecking changed from normal to an echo. The bird let out a cry louder than she had all day. The sudden cry made Willow turn around with a start. When she turned, she saw an open door to a little house. Of all the times she had been in the forest, she never noticed this before. Willow knew this forest like the back of her hand. She thought for a moment. She was seeing things due to the storm, but she kept moving forward to the entrance.

Willow's feet finally hit the threshold of the little abode. The owl was already in the home. She was hesitant about going into the house. This was not hers. She had no business entering someone's home. From the appearance of this house, it had not been occupied for quite some time. The cobwebs on the sills of the window and in the frame of the door were quite different from the web her friend had made at her house.

The house was dimly lit from the window light from outside. Willow noticed a candle, holder, and the matches by the door. She lit the candle and started her way through the little house.
It seemed that no one had lived in this house for a very long time.   The interior of the house was stone. She expected it to be dirt. Someone took a lot of time digging this house and putting the limestone in for the walls. She lit more candles so she could get a better view of the whole house.

The house looked very different in the candlelight. It was a cozy little place, even cheerful. It did need a good cleaning. Dust had taken over and it did smell stale. Life needed to be breathed into this house again. There was so much to explore with this hidden treasure. This house had secrets to tell. And the secrets were waiting to be shared.

Willow did not want to spend much time in the house in the event
someone would come along and find her. She would not have a
believable explanation of why she was in a house that was not her
own. She didn't want to be in trouble with the law for trespassing.

There was an aura about the house screaming out to her to stay a
while, to relax and listen to the storm's song inside a safe place. Willow
liked storms. They had a calming effect on her. She decided it would not
do any harm for her to linger a bit longer. After all, it was raining and she
was already wet enough for her liking.

Willow looked around the small home for something to give more
light. She wanted to explore the small house and did not want to stumble
over unseen things that would bring her physical harm. She found an
abundance of candles, holders and matches lying on a table near the
fireplace. She lit a few and started to explore the house. She was slightly
chilly, but she knew the smoke from the chimney would draw attention to
the little house. She did not want to do anything to cause
attention. Warming up by a candle would have to suffice for the time
being. It was not winter and a little chill would not harm her.

The house looked as if someone had just picked up and left. There
were dishes in the cupboards, rugs on the floor, books, furniture, and even
clothes hanging in the closet. Who lived here? Where did they go? Why
was it so hidden? All those questions kept repeating in her mind as she
walked through the house.

She went into the bedroom and found a wooden chest. She looked
around the room and felt as if someone was watching her. She knew
there was no one present at the house. She slowly bent down to open the
chest. The heavy lid creaked as if it were stretching after a long nap.

Inside the chest she found many things. There were quilts, laces,
books, and a jewelry box. Every item in the chest was preserved as if
they were placed there yesterday. She was surprised the moths didn't
have a feast of a lifetime on all the materials.
She took out the jewelry box with care and delicately ran her fingers over
the lid. It was the most beautiful thing she had ever seen. The engraved
lid of the box had a tree with every branch loaded with leaves. The leaves
were engraved with the utmost detail. Even the veins of the leaves and
the bark of the tree looked as if you were looking at a nature's real
creation. The engraving must have taken a very long time to

complete. She was in total awe of the craftmanship. You would never find anything like this for sale in the Marketplace. Even if you did, no one would be able to afford such a treasure.

Her fingers tried to open the lid without success. She wanted to see what treasures it held inside! How could someone just leave this? She tried once more to open it; again, without success. She set the box aside with disappointment and continued to explore the rest of the contents in the chest.

The quilts were made from the finest fabrics she had ever seen. The threads were not made of horsehair and other materials other quiltmakers used. These quilts were made from real thread seamstresses used in making dresses. These were grand quilts only to be used on special occasions. She looked to the bed. The beautiful quilt on the bed seemed to be used for everyday use. And there were only a few moth holes!

Willow felt a little chill travel through her body, so she wrapped the quilt around her shoulders and went on exploring. The laces were also the finest she had touched! She picked up a section of lace that had a scenery on it. This piece had a hillside with three trees, a church, and a full moon so delicately stitched into the fabric. She could see the scene in her mind. And the word exquisite came to mind.

She was almost to the bottom of the chest. There was a book. Carefully, she picked it up. The book was bound in leather. The pages were brownish yellow from either being in the trunk so long or it could have just been the color of the page. The pages were tied together with an orange ribbon and a vine. She was drawn to this book like a bat is that is drawn to the flight of night. She was ready to untie the ribbon when the sound of a horse caught her attention.

Someone is here! Someone knows about the house! Do they know she is here? She put the book under the lace and rushed to put everything back in the trunk. She quickly and carefully closed the lid. She swiftly moved to blow out the candles she had lit. She did not want to be discovered. She looked around the small house and found the darkest corner to hide in. She held her breath and prayed no one would enter the home. She feared what would happen if she were to be discovered.

With the sound of the horses taking off again, Willow let out a sign of relief. She knew the house was telling her that she had worn out her

welcome. She needed to be going back to where she belonged. She
didn't want to upset the house as she wanted to come back soon. The
house had more to tell her; but it was going to be in its own time not
hers. She did not want to force anything. She made sure all the embers
from the candles were out. Then she made her way to the door.
When she poked her head out the door, the sky let her know how much
time had passed since her friend the owl led her into the house. It was
dusk now. She didn't want to be caught in the forest at night without a
lantern. Willow knew she must hurry if she were to make it back to her
home by dark. She closed the door to the abode and made her way back
to her home smiling.

CHAPTER 6

As she was walking home, Willow found herself on autopilot. The thoughts of the house in the meadow were occupying her mind. She looked at the spider's masterpiece as she walked by. Oh, how grand it was becoming.   The intricate design reminded her so much of the beautiful lace she had found in the trunk. There were no flaws in the web just as there were no flaws in the lace. The spider was nowhere around. It must be hunting for food somewhere else. Hopefully it was not in another's web which didn't have such grace as its own.

Willow opened the door to her humble home. For some reason, it seemed different to her now. Her home seemed so much bigger in some aspects than it did when she left it hours earlier. She liked her home. It welcomed her every day with a sense of safety and security.

She realized she was hungry. The only thing she had eaten were the gooseberries she had sampled while gathering the bitter berries earlier. She was about to get something in the soup pot when there was a knock on the door.

"Hello, who's knocking at my door?"

"It is me, Adam," came an anxious voice.

"Adam?" she asked in surprised.

"Can you please open the door?"

Willow rushed to open the door. There he stood, flushed face. His eyes were the most intense color of blue she had ever seen.

"Adam, what's the matter? Why is your face so flushed?"

"Are you okay? You are not hurt, are you?" he asked, visibly shaken. He took her hands into his.

"Adam, I am fine! What has you so shaken up?"

"Are you certain you're okay? You are not hurt?"

"Yes, I am certain. Come, let's sit on the porch and you can explain to me what has you so upset," she said as she led him to the porch and motioned for him to sit down on the chairs with her.

"I was out riding today. I went into the forest, and I found your basket tipped over with gooseberries scattered. And your shoes were laying by the tree.   I called out your name several times, but you didn't answer. I became worried."

Willow didn't even realize she didn't have her shoes on. Her feet didn't ache to let her know they were missing shoes. She could see the worry in his eyes.   She didn't want to lie to him; but she couldn't let him in on her secret at this time either.

"As I was gathering gooseberries, I sat down by the tree to relax in the breeze. I had fallen asleep when the rain came in so suddenly. I stood up quickly, spilling the basket. I then made such a mad dash to seek shelter, I must have forgotten my shoes. I am a silly woman," she embellished the truth with a faint smile.

"When I saw the overturned basket and the shoes, I thought maybe an animal chose you for its next meal. I was worried. I called and called your name but didn't get a reply. I am glad you are home and safe."

"I am home now. A lesson learned to be more watchful of the weather and not to be caught in the rain again. Next time I may not be so lucky."

"Oh, I believe you could calm any storm. A storm is no match for you."

"You must not say things you don't mean.'

"Oh, one will never accuse me of saying things I don't mean."

"Beg my pardon. You must be hungry and thirsty."

"Oh, I don't want to impose."

"Not imposing at all. The least I can do for a man who is so concerned for my welfare is to feed him. I was about to put on a pot of stew. I would be quite offended if you would turn me down."

"Very well, then. I would not want to offend a lady." He chuckled.

They went inside and she got right to work on the meal. They made small talk while they ate their supper. She noticed something different about Adam this night. She noticed how very handsome he was. The light from the fire cast a perfect shadow of his face. His cheekbones were so defined when he smiled or laughed. He also had deep dimples in his cheeks when he smiled. His eyes were twinkling when he laughed. When she talked, he really listened to her. She knew this to be true as the wrinkle on his forehead showed his feelings as she spoke.

Adam was truly a handsome man. She loved the crow's feet in the corner of his eyes when he laughed or smiled. She found his presence both calming and exhilarating. She never thought one person could cause such inflictions on her heart, mind and maybe even her very soul.

He had a rugged elegance about him. Adam was not built like many of the other well-to-do men in the village. Other men with an easy-privileged life had bodies of skin and bones that reminded her of skeletons with skin and vocal abilities. Such men were not used to the elements the outside could render on a man. Hard work also was not a common practice for these men. Adam was quite different. He stood almost a foot and a half taller than she. His shoulders were broad. His arms were so strong you could see his muscles through the sleeves in his shirt. His legs were as strong as oak tree branches.   He certainly was handsome. And he could handle anything life would present to him. He did have financial means also.

At that moment in time, in the light of the candles, she realized she and Adam were not that different after all. She smiled at the thought. The smile widened when the realization came to her that he was at her house sharing a simple meal of stew and bread.

She didn't know how long they sat, talked and laughed. It felt like hours, but it was not long enough. Conversation flowed so easy between the two of them; like they would never cease to have a topic to share.

"Oh, dear! I didn't realize the crickets started singing their song! I feel I must not over extend my welcome. For if I don't go now, I will not be welcomed back," Adam apologized once he realized the time.

She felt her heart sink a little bit in her chest. She didn't want him to go just yet. "Nonsense, you are always welcome here no matter what the hour."

"All the same, I must be going. I can only imagine what people would say if I stayed much longer. I'm sure jaws will be cackling like old hens in the morning."

"We've had this discussion already. Let them talk. I don't need to prove anything to anyone. I am not concerned about what people think of me." She asserted boldly.

"Then, I must care for the both of us. Thank you for the delicious meal and the excellent conversation."

"You are most certainly welcome," she said as she opened the door for him.

"I better be going now. I am certain there are no eyes looking upon to see." He said, looking both ways before looking back at her.

Willow didn't care if the whole town was spying on her. The busy tongues didn't worry for the safety of her reputation. But it was Adam's reputation that brought her concern. No one cared about her and her name. She would be surprised if they even knew her name. Everyone knew Adam.

She didn't want him to go. She felt his hesitation also. They stood in her doorway just looking into one another's eyes. She could feel her cheeks getting pink and her heart beating a little faster in her chest. His face was getting closer to hers. He was going to kiss her! She wanted him to kiss her, more than she realized. He was just about to lean in when they were interrupted by the snort of his horse.

"Okay, Sylvester," he muttered to his horse.

"Good night, Adam. Be safe." She light-heartedly said as she watched him mount his horse and watched him ride away with a happy heart.

CHAPTER 7

Willow woke the next morning to an unusual silence. The birds were too quiet. She had a sense of overwhelming dread. She quickly dressed and went out to her porch.

She gazed around her to find nothing rushing about. Usually there were people out and starting their day. But there was nothing happening at all. She looked to the sky to see if smoke was coming from chimneys, but there was none.

She grabbed her shawl and headed towards the village. Certainly, someone there would have news of what was happening this morning. When she arrived at the village, she noticed a small crowd in front of Timothy's house.

"What brings such a crowd?" she inquired.

"It's Sarah. She woke screaming in such pain. She even scared the widow's rooster."

"Has anyone called for the doctor?"

"Yes, but he is out of town. He isn't expected to return until day after morrow. Timothy is beside himself, caring for her and the baby."

"I can only imagine."

"Is there anyone here who may be able to bring some comfort to this woman?" Mr. Wells shouted into the crowd.

The villagers looked at one another. No one moved forward or murmured a single word. They could hear Sarah's agonizing screams clearly in the silence. The screams then echoing back to remind you the hills couldn't take her pain-filled cries either. Another cry was quickly followed by an even louder one. This process continued for what seemed like forever; but in reality, was only seconds.

"Clearly you are all here out of curiosity. There is nothing to see here if you cannot provide help! Go on about your business. There is nothing to see here. Let this family be!" a familiar voice shouted through the crowd.

One by one, people dispersed and went about their daily business. Sarah's cries were getting weaker. They still sent a chill down one's spine when they were released from Sarah's throat.

"Poor Sarah," a deep voice whispered beside her.

"Adam, hello. Poor Timothy must be beside himself." Willow said, glancing at the house.

"I went to your cottage to gather and bring you here."

"Bring me here? Why?"

"To see if you can help poor Sarah," Timothy spoke up from the porch of his home.

Willow and Adam turned toward the house and she replied, "I'm not sure how I can help. I am not a doctor."

"But you helped us before," Timothy insisted.

"Oh, Timothy, that was for an upset tummy of a baby. Not screams coming from Sarah's tormented body."

"Something is better than nothing. I beg you. I cannot bear that Anna has to hear her mother in pain. Nor know I did nothing to ease her mother's pain." Timothy begged.

"That is why I came to gather you. You can help Sarah," Adam urged as he looked at her with pleading eyes.

Her thoughts were racing as hastily as the wind. Could she help Sarah? She was not a doctor, but she knew Timothy had a valid point.

"I will see what I can do. I make no promises but to try my best." She replied as she lifted her skirt and went up the porch steps to enter Timothy's house.

She rushed to Sarah's bedside. In a bed which seemed to swallow her, there laid the frail, petite woman. Her eyes closed, beads of sweat traveled down her face, and her honey hair spread out on the pillows. She was pale and her lips were busy mumbling a prayer, only to be interrupted by whimpers of pain instead of shrieks of pain.

"Sarah, someone is here to help." Timothy comforted his wife.

Sarah opened her eyes long enough to see the woman, but she said nothing to her.

"I will see what I can do. I will try the best I can. Timothy, you have my word."

"Thank you. I will leave you to your work." Timothy looked back with love and concern at his wife as he left the bedroom.

Willow took one look at the woman in the bed and could tell Sarah was very, very ill.

"Dear Lord, please help this woman. Guide my hands, mind, and my soul to help her." Willow whispered before she took a wet cloth to wipe the perspiration from Sarah's face. She lifted up Sarah's head to wipe the back of her neck when she felt a bump.

The bump was like nothing Willow had ever felt before in all her years. This bump was different than one you get when you bump your head from not paying attention to where you are going. This bump was soft on the edges and hard as if a pebble was in the middle.

Anxiety filled her body. Willow could feel her body tense like someone had just tightened her corset. She called out for the others in the house. She needed supplies if she were to care for Sarah to the best of her ability.

"Timothy, heat some water. We will need some to drink and some for use. Please get a fresh rag soaked with the warm water. Also, find a needle in Sarah's sewing basket." Continuing her instructions, she requested, "Adam, please go to my cottage. Get a gold pouch and a clear bottle with rough salt rocks." The men did as they were instructed.

Anna was a beautiful baby girl. The Lord truly blessed Timothy and Sarah with this little one. At Willow's age, she had never been around a lot of babies, or even been around a lot of children. But being left alone with Anna at this moment, she was not nervous at all.
Sarah was only a year older than she. Sarah was a wife and a mother already. Before she knows it, Sarah will be rocking her grandchildren to a peaceful slumber in the same rocking chair Willow was now sitting in. She felt a hint of jealousy; but it quickly left. Willow knew her destiny was still unfolding. The Good Lord had a plan for her. At this present time, she knew her destiny was to do what she could so Timothy and Sarah could grow old together and Anna would grow up with a mother.

"I gathered the things as soon as I could. What's wrong with my wife?" Timothy asked, breathlessly as he interrupted her from her thoughts.

"Great, thank you. Now we wait for Adam." She said as she rose from the chair to gaze out the window. She purposedly avoided answering Timothy's question.

"I pray he can find what he needs."

"He will. His horse is fast. Time always stands still when it's competing with our hearts and minds."

"I will go check on the kettles. I don't want the water to be too hot." Timothy babbled before leaving the room.

"Two more bottles to the right. Yes, that one. The gold pouch. No that's bronze. The gold. Move to the right. Yes. You have it. Now hurry." She said to herself in her mind, picturing Adam in her house.

"Adam will be here shortly." She informed Timothy as he entered the room.

"I have two kettles of water ready. The rag is soaking up the warmth of the water in one of them. I dropped the needle. I need to go find another. Hopefully I can locate one before Adam returns," he stammered.

Adam burst through the door and Timothy rushed to find a new needle.

She began her instructions to each of the men. "Okay, I need someone to put a pinch of what is in the gold pouch into a cup and steep for a drink. Also, I need someone to mix a stick that looks like tree bark that is in the pouch to just enough of what is in the bottle to make a paste. Then place the paste on a small section of the cloth. Cut the cloth in tiny squares. I need the needle, please."

"I cannot find another needle! What do you need the needle for?" Timothy panicked.

"I need to release this sore's anger." She informed him as she lifted up Sarah's hair to reveal a boil as big around as a coin. It was raised like a small anthill you would find on the ground. The wound was fiercely angry. The bump's fury was beginning to fester to where little crimson lines were venturing from the center to deep red lines down her neck. She knew she had to calm this lesion down or it would be deadly.

"Oh God, help us!" she heard Adam exclaim.

"What caused that horrid thing!" Timothy gasped.

"Right now, I need to release the anger from it. I need the needle to puncture it. I'm going to release the poison so I can then put the paste on the open wound to draw out the rest of the anger. We don't have much time, Timothy. I need the paste and a needle."

Adam knew Sarah was in grave danger. The red streaks were visible on the skin of her neck, but not visible if they were going to her brain. Timothy stood like a statue in a garden. Adam knew he had to do something. He would not allow this woman to die leaving a child motherless like he was. As long as he was in that bedroom, Adam was going to do something. In one swift move he grabbed one of Sarah's hair pins, put it in the flame of the candle for a few seconds, blew on it to cool and handed it to Willow. The two exchanged glances before Willow did what must be done.

"Lord, please steady my hand to do good. Please release the anger from this woman's wound and body." Willow prayed before she stuck the pin into the center of the wound.

When the pin entered the center of the wound, only a small amount of whitish-yellow liquid came oozing from the opened source. The fiery infection was not going to leave Sarah's body easily. Willow took the pin and punctured Sarah's skin several more times to form a circle of tiny holes around the center of the wound. Tiny streams of white puss escaped the circle, but not enough; and it surely was not quickly enough.

"I don't understand, why isn't it working?" Timothy pleaded.

"The infection has taken quite a liking to Sarah. Thankfully it hasn't spread to her whole body. I am going to do a couple more things. She will not die tonight."

"What happens next?" Adam asked.

"I will squeeze the anger out of the wound. I will need a cloth with the paste so it can be applied when I am done."

Willow turned Sarah's neck to where she could see the wound clearly. The infection was trickling down her neck like dew on a window on a cold morning.

Willow soothingly spoke to Sarah as she placed her hands on Sarah's neck. "Sarah, I am going to squeeze hard on this sore. Scream if need be; my ears will be able to bear it. I will try my best to be gentle."

She exchanged looks with Timothy, who was trying his best not to pace the floor, then Adam, who was paying close attention to her every move. She then took a deep breath and proceeded with the task at hand.

When Willow placed her thumbs on the sides of the wound, she could feel the infection building in the little space. The wound was as warm as an angry man's face, like Mr. Wells in the Marketplace, She knew the warmer the wound became, the more danger Sarah was in. The more of a home the infection was going to make in her body, the more it may never leave.

She gave a gentle squeeze. As she did, she could feel the liquid shift from the outer edge to the middle of the wound. White, thick liquid like the milk from a milkweed plant came out of the little holes. Willow was relieved to see more of the poison be expelled. She squeezed harder the second time and even more liquid came out. It actually squirted out and landed on her arm.

"I need the cloth with the paste on it, please."

Timothy quickly handed her the cloth, not taking his eyes off of Sarah for a single second. His face showed a small bit of relief as he looked at the puss on the rag and the size of the wound on his wife's neck.

"This cloth needs to remain on the wound overnight. She may tell you it hurts or stings a bit, but this needs to stay on the wound. Timothy, this **must** stay on the wound." She instructed sternly.

"What does the paste do? Why will it hurt her? I don't want her in more pain."

"The paste will draw out the poison that is in her body. I wouldn't do anything to deliberately cause Sarah pain. I would take the pain myself so she wouldn't suffer. Needless to say, even spare Anna's young ears from taking her mother's screams." That said, she placed the cloth squares on Sarah's neck.

"Forgive me if I sounded accusatory," a tired and worried husband's voice came across rudely. "Please forgive me. I am quite ashamed." Timothy said regretfully, bowing his head.

"I didn't take offense, Timothy. No need to apologize for loving your wife. I can see you are tired. You need to rest. Go rest and I will watch little Anna."

"Oh, that is the most generous of you, but I must decline."

"This woman you trust with your wife, but not your child? Watch your words, Timothy." Adam defended the woman.

"Adam…" Willow started to speak.

"No! You are the only one out of the village who even stepped forth to help a woman's screams who could wake the dead! How dare he speak to you this way?"

"Adam, it is quite the opposite. For the reasons you speak are the exact reason why I cannot allow her to care for dear Anna. Willow has acted unselfishly by helping my dear Sarah. She, and you, have spent much time here. I do not claim to be a smart man when it comes to women. But I do know when a woman is tired. She has given too much of herself already." Timothy explained with a weary smile.

"Timothy, I am quite alright. You need to rest."

"See, Anna is getting sleepy. I will rock her and she will be asleep in no time. Sarah is quiet and sleeping now. Go along, I will be fine." Timothy explained as he picked Anna up in his arms and began to rock her in the chair.

Willow studied Timothy's eyes to see if the words he spoke were falsehood or truth. His eyes were red from tears, tired and weary from exhaustion and worry; but he spoke the true and heartfelt words.

"Come, Adam. Let's leave this family to have a good night's slumber." Willow said as she stood up, stretched over to Timothy's arms and lightly touched Anna's cheek.

"Many thanks to the both of you. We shall sleep well tonight."

"We will return tomorrow." Adam spoke to Willow's surprise.

Willow's thoughts were confused. We? Did he just say we? We, as in he and she? He probably said we by a slip of the tongue, after all it has been a stressful few hours.

"Yes, tomorrow," she quickly regained her wits. "Keep the cloth on her neck. If she starts to be in pain again, come and get me. She should sleep until the infection has escaped her wound, at least most of it. The wound was very angry, please keep an eye on it. I will leave you until the morning. God bless." She comforted as she hugged him.

"May God shed many blessings upon you both." Timothy said, shaking Adam's hand and smiling for the first time in hours.

CHAPTER 8

The daylight had evaporated while she had been tending to Sarah. Willow and Adam stepped out on to Timothy's porch just in time to see the day's masterpiece of red, orange, blue and a sliver of purple spread across the western horizon. The temperature was typical for the autumn season. She inhaled the fall air with vigor. It was nice to breathe in the fresh air. The air inside Timothy's home was growing stale as a house of the ill often tends to become. She couldn't wait to go home and relax with a cup of tea and a meal.

"You must be hungry," Adam spoke, breaking her stream of thoughts.

"I've been so busy I hadn't given food a thought."

"My stomach is telling me it's in need of food. Come and join me for a meal."

"I am not dressed to go anywhere but home. I must look a fright." She groaned, embarrassed of how disheveled she must have looked.

"Then let me walk you home and I shall do the cooking tonight." He gave her a smile.

"You are too kind. You look weary. I can walk home by myself. You go and rest."

"I should not sleep a wink. I would be awake with worry not knowing if you had made it home safely."

She could feel her face blushing. She was thankful for the lack of sun so Adam couldn't see her embarrassment and excitement. She could feel her body start to tingle wildly. He took her hand and they started walking. She felt a jolt of electricity rush through her body. Normally she would have pulled her hand away. But she didn't want to offend him. She liked the joy it gave her.

The pair didn't speak much on the brief walk to her house. The only sound in the still of the evening came from Adam's horse, which seemed glad to be free of the weight of a passenger. The couple walked contentedly. The truth of the matter was, they were getting warmer and warmer with each passing minute. Adam still had a firm grip on her hand. She could feel his heartbeat through his hand slow and steady, unlike hers.

Willow's thoughts started to run away with her. *"Oh no! Can he feel the rapid beating of my heart? Should I pull away? Oh, I couldn't. It would offend him greatly."* She took a deep breath and tried to calm herself.

"So here we are at last." He announced as they stopped in front of her cottage.

"So we are."

"Let's go inside so I can cook dinner for you. Your stomach will become angry if I don't," he remarked as he led her up the steps of her front porch.

"Let's," she agreed.

Once inside, Adam directed her to a chair at the kitchen table. "Sit down and relax. I will be the one doing the cooking tonight."

"What is that most delicious smell? I think I smell baked chicken and apples," she asked as the aromas filled her senses.

"The smell that entertains your nose is supper."

"When? How?" She asked with curiosity.

"A great chef does not reveal his secrets," he teased, touching her on the tip of her nose.

"Oh, I beg your pardon, dear sir," she laughingly responded.

"Take a rest. It should be ready soon," he noted as he handed her a cup of her favorite tea. She looked at the cup. It was indeed her favorite tea. She didn't even realize he knew her favorite tea. And it was in her favorite cup. She took the cup and sat at her table.

She watched him do what she should be doing for him. She watched him taste test the meal, making sure it was suitable to eat. She was confident by the smells filling her nose that the food would be delicious. The food could be baked worms and mud, for all she cared. She wouldn't mind as long as it was made by his hands and she had his company.

The meal was ready quickly. The two ate and carried on with easy pleasant conversation. The conversation was not forced with the two of them. It came as natural to them as breathing.

"I see the moon is making her presence known and Sylvester is growing restless." Adam acknowledged as the horse made his presence known.

"He has been very patient today. He has also been very busy. You should reward him with an apple, carrot, or extra oats upon arriving home."

"I shall give him all three."

"It will be a just and well-deserved reward."

"You are a sly one. I'm sure Sylvester thanks you." He quipped as they stepped outside.

They walked down the stairs together. As soon as her feet hit the soil, Willow's body became tense. The night did not hold the familiarities it normally held. Something felt amiss. She quickly looked around but saw nothing out of place. All seemed as it should be at night.

"Thank you for the wonderful meal and the extraordinary company." She said contently before petting Sylvester on his nose.

"The pleasure is all mine." He replied as he mounted the steed with ease.

"The moon is full and I hear the wolves. Please avoid the forest tonight," she warned.

"I am sure my journey home will be uneventful. Until tomorrow. Sleep well."

"Do you have your pistol?" Willow asked with concern.

Adam felt for the weapon but noticed it was not in the holster. He remembered he had placed it on the kitchen table when he was cooking the meal. He jumped off the horse in one swift move and went into the house to gather the weapon.

"Listen carefully, my dear friend," Willow whispered in the animal's ear. "Gallop swiftly to your home, to safety. Do not be afraid, for you are protected."

"Are you plotting against me?"

"No. I was just telling Sylvester that an apple, a carrot and extra oats were promised to him for his patience and loyalty." She smiled as she caressed the animal's nose.

"Well, now I have to do it. I would not want him to think the beautiful lady speaks lies. Come on, old boy. Let's get home and get your rewards," he said as she turned the horse loose to go home.

"Moon be his light. Guard him safe home this night. Keep him out of harm's way and him back here at the light of day." She requested of the moon before going inside.

Willow prepared herself for bed reflecting on her day. Her mind traveled to Sarah and her illness. There were no wails coming from their home so slumber must have found the home at last.

She prayed the angry wound on Sarah's neck would not be plaguing her anymore or in the near future. Willow had never seen a wound get so angry so quickly. She would have wait until the morning to see what mood the sore would present itself.

The hoot of the owl and symphony of the crickets were telling her it was time for herself to slumber. She finished preparing herself for bed, blew out the candle beside her bed and stared out the window at the almost full moon. She smiled at the thought of what both the full moon and her dreams would bring.

Slumber was not her friend this night. Her dreams were plagued with Adam. Usually dreaming of him would bring a sense of calm and serenity, but not this night. Her dreams produced feelings quite the opposite.

In this dream, Adam was being chased by a group of men. Sylvester was galloping as if the Devil's horse itself was chasing the pair.

"Keep your pace, dear friend!" Adam encouraged his faithful mount. The horse snorted as if to reply, seeming to understand his master's words. The steed picked up the pace as he had never done in all the years Adam had owned him.

"Skies of night, Sun of light, make this man disappear from sight. The men who wish him harm will be no match for this charm." Willow heard a voice say as a charm was shown being held in the palms of a woman's hands that were not her own.

"Winds hear my words. See my hands. Do what my words command. Show your fury. Show your anger. Keep Adam safe from danger. Let your hurry fiercely blow. May his enemies never know." The woman chanted as she made actions with her hands that could not be made out in the dream.

The winds in the dream blew like Willow never seen them before. She could see the branches of the trees bend at the demands of the woman. The birds and other night animals ceased their songs and flights. Fog rolled in to cover the land like a blanket out of nowhere hiding the lady to where Willow could only make out a silhouette of a thin woman with long hair flowing in the wind.

There was no moonlight or starlight to aid in seeing the woman more clearly. The only light was coming from the charm she was holding in her hands. There were streams of gold coming from the coin. Willow tried to look again, but no luck. The three streams of light were the brightest she had ever seen.

The woman was speaking to her; but the words were silent. Willow tried to talk to her but no words were audible coming from her either. It was as if someone stole her words once they entered her mind. If their conversation was audible, they would not be able to hear each other due to the screams of the hurricane-like winds.

The dream-slumber came back with Adam and Sylvester finally reaching home. The winds calmed as soon as Sylvester was safe in his stable with the extra apple, carrots and oats just like Willow instructed both man and beast.

CHAPTER 9

The morning song of the birds disturbed her sleep earlier than she would have liked. Willow was both intrigued and fearful of the previous night's dream. She wondered what it meant. Who was the woman? Why did the woman come to her? What was the woman's connection to Adam?

Adam! Her thoughts ran immediately to him. Willow had to know if he was safe. She knew she couldn't go to his house. His father would surely turn her away. She quickly got dressed and closed her eyes.

"I close my eyes, but help me see, the one I desire, blessed be." She uttered to herself. In her mind, she saw Adam at his house preparing go come to town. She gave a sigh of relief. Willow could feel the stress and worry evaporate from her body like water in a puddle on a hot day.

Memories from her dream were not going to totally escape her this day. She tried to put them in the back of her mind. She remembered the events of the previous day and night; for those were the events she knew were real. Her relief didn't last long. There was a rushed pounding on her door. She could tell by the urgency of the pounding the person on the other side must be in need of dire assistance.

Willow rushed to the door and opened it to find no one standing at her door. She glanced around outside to find nothing nor anyone who could have knocked. She looked beside the stairs and noticed the spider was still working at her masterpiece.

She gazed towards Timothy's house. Willow needed to go check on Sarah. She grabbed some herbs in her jar and pouches in her cabinet and started towards Timothy's house.

The heat of the sun was warm on her face. She smiled at the warmth for she knew the bitter cold would be here soon. When Willow arrived in the village, the scene was quite different than the morning before. It was busy, which was a welcomed sight but the energy of the townspeople and air was calmer.

Willow arrived at Timothy and Sarah's home to find Anna playing on the porch and Timothy having a cup of coffee.

"Good morning! Hi Anna!" She greeted as she played with the little girl.

"Hello, Willow. How are you this fine morning?"

"I am well, thank you. I came to check on Sarah."

"I can't thank you enough. Would you like a cup of coffee or tea perhaps?"

"Thank you, but I will pass. May I go in to see Sarah?"

"Of course." Timothy opened the door for her.

Sarah was up in bed. She had a bit more color in her cheeks than the day before. Her face and arms were not covered with sweat as they were the night before. Humming had replaced the wails of pain from her throat.

"Willow, come in, please. I thought I heard your voice." Sarah cheerfully invited her into the room.

"Hello, Sarah. I won't linger long as you need your rest."

"Don't be foolish! You can stay as long as you wish. Come sit, let's visit." Sarah smiled.

Willow did as she was instructed. She sat on the same stool Timothy occupied the night before while sitting vigil.

"Can I look at your wound? It was quite angry last evening. I hope Timothy kept the bandage on it." Willow stated.

"Oh, I assure you, Timothy followed your directions to the letter. I wanted to take it off, but he insisted I leave it on until you came back." She beamed with fondness for her husband.

"He is a good man. He loves you very much. Now, let's take a look at your wound." Willow said as she took the bandage off of Sarah's neck.

The wound was still angry. The infection did seep onto the white cloth leaving a yellowish-green stain on the cloth.   The wound had a white lump the size of a small fingertip. The crimson lines were less red, almost a pink color against Sarah's beautiful white skin.

"Is it gone?" Sarah asked.

"No. The red lines traveling out are now pink. There is a large red bump with the anger in the center rising. I will need to release it again and put the bandage back on the wound. It is healing nicely. Have you been drinking the tea I gave Timothy?"

"Yes, I have. It tastes very good. What do you have to do to the wound? I don't have a headache anymore. Can we just let the paste do the work?"

"The paste will help. But the wound must be drained of the poison or it will never heal. The paste will be a slow healing process and your headaches will certainly come back. If I poke it again with a pin, more infection will be released. The sooner the wound and your body comes to an agreement, the sooner you can be up and about with your family," Willow explained to her friend.

Sarah sat in her bed and looked at Willow. She was doubting her friend's words. The first time Sarah was in too much pain to care or to make decisions.

"You doubt my words?"

"I do."

"I would not do anything I wouldn't do for myself. I would not do anything to chance Anna being left without a mother or Timothy without a wife." Willow defended herself, feeling hurt.

"I understand. Please, I didn't mean to offend. I am so thankful for all you have done and will do for me and my family. I would just like one more day with the paste and the bandage. I fear needles." Sarah explained.

"Very well. I won't go against your wishes at this time. I will get a clean bandage and prepare the paste."

"Thank you, Willow, for understanding."

"You're welcome. I will return in a few minutes." Willow replied as she left the room.

"How is the wound? Is it still angry?" Timothy asked as soon as Willow came into view.

"Yes, but not as much. There is a bump with a mound of infection. She won't let me poke it like I did last night. She wants to put the paste and bandage on the wound. Do you still have the remainder of the paste?"

"Yes. There is more paste as I didn't put any more of it on the bandage after you left last night. Is it wise to do it this way? To not release the anger?"

"It may not be the wisest for healing; but it is what Sarah requested to be done."

"You need to talk her into letting you do what you feel is best!" He panicked.

"Timothy, Sarah is a strong woman who knows what she wants. My words will fall on deaf ears. I will prepare the bandage," she explained to him.

"Very well," came Timothy's simple reply.

Willow made the paste and bandage with ease. She looked at Anna who was napping in her wooden cradle. She smiled at the sleeping baby. Anna was destined for great things. Willow could feel it in her bones.

Heading back to the bedroom, Willow stated to both Sarah and Timothy, "Same instructions as before. Keep this on the wound. It will hurt as the wound is angry and festering. If the red lines appear or you start to get headaches or dizzy, call for me and I will come straight away. I will not be in the village the rest of the day; but I shall return home by the end of the day." She gave them both a stern look.

"Thank you. Have a blessed day." Sarah said with a smile.

"Many thanks and blessings to you." Timothy thanked.

"You are most welcome. Please do what I instructed. The wound is unpredictable until healed. I will see you tomorrow or the day after." With that, Willow left the young family and headed down the steps to the street.

Willow was going to walk into the village to see what was happening in town; however, she chose to go home instead. She wanted to check her garden and then pick berries for some pies. She also realized she never made it to the meadow the other day. She found herself skipping with excitement at the thought of being in the meadow again.

In a short time, her house was in sight. She saw a familiar figure on her porch. She smiled with glee! Her feet took her from a skip to a sprint, only to stop when she leaped into his open arms.

"Well, that is quite a welcome!" he chuckled as he hugged her tightly.

"Are my eyes playing tricks on me? Am I seeing you in the flesh and not being tricked by my dreams?" she asked.

"It is no vision or deception. I am here in the flesh, dear one."

"I can hardly believe it! Come inside for some food and drink as you must be parched and hungry," she led him in the house so fast his legs could hardly move fast enough.

"The journey was long, that is true."

"Then come, relax." She chattered as she practically shoved him into a chair.

"You look well, dear one."

"I am trying. You look too thin," she observed touching his cheek.

"I eat."

"But do you eat well and often?" she questioned.

"Well…." he answered laughing.

"I thought as much. Eat this. It is not much but it will hold you over until supper," she said as she sat a plate of ham, potatoes, and pie in front of him.

"It is plenty. Aren't you going to join me? It's rude for a cook not to eat her own cooking, especially in front of her guest."

She quickly made herself a plate and joined her visitor. She knew arguing with him would be pointless and she was hungry.

"Willow, I must tell you something." He began before there was a knock at the door.

"Who is it?" Willow asked.

"It's Adam."

"Hello, Adam."

"Come in," she welcomed as she opened the door.

Adam was taken aback by the sight of a man sitting at Willow's table. He was curious as to who and why this man was at the table. And most of all, could this man be trusted? Adam quickly dismissed the thought of mistrust. He knew Willow would never invite a man she could not trust into her home and offer him food and drink.

"Oh goodness! Where are my manners? Adam, this is Joseph. Joseph is a cousin of mine who decided to surprise me with a visit. Joseph, this is Adam, a dear friend of mine." She introduced the two men. She could feel her cheeks getting warm once again.

"Welcome to Baxter," Adam greeted as he extended his hand for Joseph to shake.

"Thank you. Willie has nothing but good things to say about the village. I wanted to check it out myself," Joseph said as he took Adam's hand. Adam seemed a bit taken aback by Joseph's use of Willow's nickname.

"Well, I hope our little village doesn't disappoint you. Where are you traveling from?"

"I am from a village some miles west of here. I am traveling east. I can't stay long. I wanted to make sure I saw Willie while I was passing this way." Joseph explained.

"Willow is lucky to have such a thoughtful cousin. I see you are sharing a meal. I apologize for the intrusion. I will be going." Adam excused himself as he headed toward the door.

"No, please stay. There is plenty, as you can see. I already made you a plate. You wouldn't want to disappoint me in front of my cousin, would you?" Willow pleaded as she sat a plate at an empty chair at the table. Adam knew he couldn't argue with her. The plate did look appetizing and the smell was like heaven. Only when he took his fork and placed it in his mouth did he think he was in heaven.

"Willie could talk anyone into anything. Even as kids, she could talk her way out of anything," Joseph laughed.

"Yes, Willow can talk anyone into anything. She's very bewitching. I bet you could share some incredible stories about our hostess," Adam chuckled before taking another bite.

"Now, now. There will be no stories told about me on this night. I'm sure you two can find something more interesting than the topic of me to converse about over a meal." She smiled as she reprimanded the men as she refilled their cups.

"Perhaps another time." Adam grinned at her.

"Sounds like a great time." Joseph agreed.

The three continued to eat and have great conversations that didn't involve any of Willow's childhood stories. They laughed until their stomachs ached. Time flew by like a bird flying south to escape the cold.

"Oh my, look at the time. I've wasted over half your day. You both must have more productive things to do besides talking to me," Joseph exclaimed.

"Meeting a new friend is never a waste of time," Adam announced.

"I agree," Willow said approvingly.

"How about you two show me around this fantastic village."

"I would love too!" Willow said with excitement in her voice like a little kid.

"I'm going to have to pass. But you have the best guide right here." Adam beamed as he touched her shoulder with praise.

"Are you sure you can't join?" Willow asked with disappointment.

"Yes, I have some business to tend to soon. Joseph came to see you. We will talk later," Adam replied and gave her a reassuring smile.

"It was nice to meet you." Joseph stood to shake his new friend's hand.

"Likewise. Next time we will share an ale and you can tell me those stories," Adam added as he winked at Willow, making her blush slightly.

Adam departed leaving Willow embarrassed. Her pink cheeks couldn't deny what she was feeling. Joseph was satisfied with the new friend he made. He knew he could trust Adam and trust wasn't something a man could easily find in a person.

CHAPTER 10

"Okay, now, I need you to tell me the real reason you are here." Willow demanded as soon as the door shut behind Adam.

"I never could hide anything from you, could I?" Joseph said with a coy smile.

"No. So don't start now," She ordered, giving him a stern look.

"I did come here because I miss you. But you are correct. There is another reason why I am here to see you after so long."

"Fine, tell me. Is it something big, Joseph? Are you in danger?" Willow asked with concerned.

"No. The fear I feel is not for me, dear one. It is you I fear who is in danger."

"Me?" she asked in shocked.

"Yes."

"Have you foreseen the future?"

"Not exactly. My visions are unclear."

"I see the fear in your eyes and hear the urgency in your voice. I believe your words."

"Dear One, heed my warning. I know details are vague and little, but the feeling is strong. Be careful who you trust, for they will be like a venomous snake and you will be its prey."

"I will. Thank you, Joseph." Willow replied as her mind began to wonder as to the meaning of his warning and the feeling he had received.

"Dear One, it will come to you when the time is right. Do not stress too much, but please be cautious."

"Enough talk about doom and gloom. Come with me," she prodded as she grabbed his hand.

"Wait! We need a lantern. It will surely be dark soon."

"Joseph, no lantern is needed, for the light provided by the moon will suffice. Now let's go while the sun still provides us with its light."

She grabbed his hand and ran as if they were seven years old. The wind Mother Earth provided them felt good with the heat from the sun. They made their way to the meadow. The meadow provided peace and comfort to her. She hoped Joseph would feel the same.

The beautiful meadow welcomed the pair as if they were coming home from a long journey. The wildflowers wrapped around them as if they were giving them a long-awaited hug. The sweet fragrance made Willow and Joseph feel alive. The two of them felt so free with no cares in the world. Most of all, they did not feel impending doom. The only emotions that radiated from them was the purest joy and love one human could feel at the present moment in time. The air was filled with their laughter. They laughed so hard and they collapsed into the soft bed the meadow grasses provided.

"I hope no one has spying eyes to see us act so foolishly," Joseph gasped.

"Oh, let them look. People see what they want to see," Willow answered as she smelled one of the small yellow wildflowers.

"You have no worries of others' opinions? Others' perceptions?" Joseph asked with concerned.

"Do the stars ask the moon how bright they may shine at night? Does the morning dew ask the grass if it can grace it with its splendor? Do the birds worry during a storm?" she asked with unshakeable calmness in her voice.

"Your words are so assured. But I will remind you, the serpent talked Eve into a dangerous deception. The end result affected all mankind. Lucifer was once an angel."

"Dear Joseph, are you comparing me to the snake or Lucifer?"

"No, Dear One. I am saying, please don't be confused. I am merely saying the words and actions of some can be quite deceiving. Peoples' minds can easily be swayed."

"I agree. People fear what they do not understand. People who choose not to understand me then it's their choice to live in fear over faith."

"I admire your way of thinking. I hope to aspire to your ways," he complimented.

"The only person you need to aspire to be is yourself." she smiled as she smelled another wildflower."

"This place is beautiful," Joseph said, changing the subject.

"I love it here. It is so calming. One can find excitement and solace here at the same time. It can bring both thoughts of clarity and chaos."

"Truly a treasure."

"Just wait until the moon and stars make their appearance."

"Truly beautiful, I'm sure," he answered in almost a whisper.

"Tell me about your adventures," Willow prompted as she propped herself up on an elbow.

"Nothing to tell, really," he contemplated as he twirled a flower in his hand.

"That is hard to believe. You always find adventure," she said looking up at the sky.

"I believe one doesn't find adventure; adventure finds you," Joseph remarked in almost a dreamy voice.

"Agreed. Life would be pretty bland without a few adventures," she replied matter-of-factly.

"Bland? What an odd choice of word," he smiled.

"When something is bland, you add spice to it. So, when life is bland, you add spice to it; hence adventure," she explained.

"Then I say, spice it up! But dear one, you will never have that problem," Joseph laughed.

"Both a blessing and a curse."

"Oh, make no mistake, you will never be cursed. Anyone who dares tries to lay a curse upon you, I pray for their souls. Anyone who meets you is surely blessed."

"Your words are too kind."

"My words are true."

The two looked at each other as if trying to read one another's thoughts. Joseph felt her confidence and strength. She felt fear in him-- life or death fear. The tremendous fear made her body shiver in the hot sun.

"I sense a great fear in you, Joseph. Please tell me what has rattled you so much," Willow asked as she held his face in her hands.

"I could never lie to you."

"Stop stalling."

"I'm in danger, dear one."

"What type of danger?"

"The kind that will find my neck stretched on the branch of a tree."

"Oh heavens. Joseph, what did you do?"

"I made some predictions. Predictions which came true. I am wanted for questioning."

"Joseph, don't spare words to save my feelings. You must tell me the truth, all of it, no matter how hard it is to say or for me to hear."

"I am wanted for witchcraft."

"Do the accusers have proof?"

"Dear one, they don't need hard proof. The words from the mouth seep into the mind."

"Oh dear."

"I fear that by coming here, I have put you in extreme danger."

"I am not worried."

"Dear One, you are so confident. But these hunters are ruthless."

"So am I. We need to worry about you," she asserted as she took his hands in hers.

"The moon and stars are making their appearance. Nothing like the light of a full moon," Joseph said with melancholy in his voice.

"Yes, there is nothing like the light of the full moon," she mumbled.

"S-h-h-h-h-h! Do you hear it? The thunder of horses' hooves, not just one but the thunder of many."

"Stay calm."

"The light of the moon will give me away! You must run. Leave me to my fate. If you stay, we will endure the same fate. If you go, your fate will be quite different," Joseph spoke with a sense of urgency.

The sounds of the horses were getting faster and closer by the second. Willow listened for any familiar voices she could recognize. However; the voices were jumbled because of shouting at the same time. The riders would be approaching fast. She needed to think of something quickly to save both of their lives.

"Where are you, Warlock! Devil!" a shout pierced the darkness. The voice was one she didn't fully recognize.

She looked up at the sky. She could see the clouds moving. This would lead the moon to shine its light on everything, making an escape impossible and bring certain tragedy.

"Take my hand!" Willow ordered as she outstretched her hand to him.

"You mustn't! What if it doesn't work!"

"You must trust me and the Universe."

Joseph took her hand and they closed their eyes. They each could feel their heartbeats through their joined hands. She had never done anything so powerful before. She prayed it would work. For she knew if it didn't, there would be two nooses on the hanging tree.

"In night in the moon's light and under the stars, let all forget who we are. All memories have gone away, in the light of the new day." She quietly spoke before the wind started to make the flowers and trees dance.

The world around them started to spin, slowly at first. Then it quickly picked up speed as the wind blew harder. She tried to keep a hold of Joseph's hand. The wind was stronger than any wind she had ever experienced in her life.

"Take this, my dear one! Something to remember me by." He implored as the wind blew harder.

There was a clap of thunder seemingly loud enough to hurt them. Then a bolt of lightning seemed to strike between their two hands and make them let go of one another in the massive winds. She looked up at the sky and saw the clouds had parted. Then suddenly, all was quiet in the meadow, as if time was frozen for just a few seconds. Not even the crickets were singing their song.

PART TWO
CHANGES ON THE HORIZON

CHAPTER 11

Willow jolted awake with a fierce start as if she was struck by lightning. Every bone and muscle in her body brutally reminded her she spent the night on her hard floor beside her fireplace instead of her warm bed.

The ashes in the fireplace proved the length of time she had been slumbering was long enough for the logs to be turned to embers causing a chill to set in the cottage. She stoked the embers and put another small log on the fire. The cottage should quickly warm.

She brushed dirt and leaves from her dress with her hands. Willow noticed mud between her fingers and under her long fingernails. She thought that was peculiar. She didn't remember that it hadn't rained the night before. She had not been working in her garden.

She looked at her reflection in the mirror to find a disturbing sight looking back at her. Her tresses appeared as if a flock of birds started to make their home in it. Her hair was, down, which she thought odd since she only let it down when she got herself ready for bed. Besides the leaves and twigs in her hair, she quite liked it down. She smiled at the reflection of her wavy locks being down. She was, however, confused on how haggard her appearance looked. Why was there mud on her dress, hands and fingernails? Why is her hair down and look such a fright?

Willow looked around the cottage to gather clues on what may have happened prior to her waking up on her floor. The cottage looked just like she remembered leaving it. No signs of having company or any unwelcomed visitors.

The cottage was not big. It had a big room that held the visiting room, kitchen, dining room and the back held a bedroom and an extra room. The large, oak door had crescent moon and star and opened to the visiting room. The floor was dirt at one time; but now was covered in wood all through the small dwelling. There were tiny windows on each wall to allow the light from both the sun and the moon.

On the back wall was a fireplace made of limestone. The stone was a perfect match of white and gray. And, if one looked hard enough, it matched the shimmer of the exterior of the cottage. The mantle of the fireplace was constructed of a chunk of an old oak tree. She was not sure of the exact origin of the tree, but she knew it had a powerful energy. On top of her mantle was a jar of simple wildflowers from nearby meadow and hand-dipped candles.

The kitchen had a square wooden table with four chairs and shelves that held bottles of herbs, liquids, and many other necessities she may need to do her work. She also had places for her dishes and pots in the small kitchen. There was a window in the kitchen also.

Her bedroom had a simple bed, a bedside table, a chest to put special things, a clothing chest, a smaller fireplace, and another window.

A modest home. A simple home. But Willow was not a woman who desired much. She was a woman who knew what she wanted and was not afraid to go after it. She was very independent. She liked this quality very much. Many loved that about her and, of course, many despised her for the quality. The greatest satisfaction was, she didn't give a damn what people thought of her. Not in the least.

At that moment, Willow wanted to get the mud off her and make a cup of tea. She put her kettle on for the tea and water in the pot on the fireplace for a bath. A cup of tea and a lavender bath were always two things to bring serenity and made her feel better instantly.

She quickly drank her tea then soaked in the fragrant, steaming hot water for a long time. She closed her eyes and tried to remember what events led to her to wake up on her floor. She had not been into the spirits or had company. She tried to remember; but her memory was keeping secrets from her for the time being. She decided it was not worth her energy to try to remember. It would all be remembered soon enough.

Willow rose from the bath, dried off, and wrapped a robe around herself. She made another cup of tea then dressed for the day in a plain, light pink dress with silver buttons. She started to put her hair up but decided to leave it down. It looked much better down, without the leaves and the twigs. The birds would have to find another place to build their nest. When she finished getting dressed, she noticed the dimness of the cottage.

"Et ent lux." She stated with open arms and a smile.

The room suddenly filled with bright light from the many candles which were placed in various places in the cottage. The many flames danced differently on their wicks. The fiery flames danced a joyful, peaceful dance. A joyful, calm flame was a good and encouraging omen. She looked at the flames one by one. Each greeted her in their own unique way, which brought her comfort.

"Dance your dance to your own melody, my dear ones!" She commented and sat down to enjoy yet another cup of her tea.

The cottage and its surroundings were quiet. She didn't mind the silence. It was comforting to her mind and her soul. Everyone needs silence in order to quiet and calm their minds and soul.

Her silence was interrupted by the sound of horses and a carriage. Willow always had people coming to her house asking for her assistance with different matters. But she didn't recognize the sound of this carriage or the horses. She sat in her chair and just listened. The hooves were not signaling danger or anger. The sound of the hooves was uncertain. Someone who had lost their way.

She made her way to the door.

"May I help you?" she asked as soon as the carriage came to a stop in front of her cottage.

"I am sorry for the intrusion. I am afraid I have lost my way." the driver of the carriage explained, embarrassed.

"No need to be sorry. We all get lost every once in a while. Where are you heading," she commented with a smile.

"Baxter."

"Oh, you just missed the turn, that is all. You need to turn around here and take a right at Bethany Creek. Then keep straight on that road and you will enter right into the village. I hope you and your passengers find Baxter to your liking and enjoyment."

"If everyone is as nice as you, I am sure we will. Thank you and good day." The driver replied as he tipped his hat to her.

"Thank you. Blessed travels." She acknowledged with a smile.

The carriage turned around. She knew by the decorations on the carriage, the passengers were not from this area. The carriage did not belong to a laborer. The carriage was a dark blue like the night. The brass medallions could outshine the sun. The spokes on the wheels were shinier than any wax produced by the finest candles in this area. The

horses were dressed in tack she had only seen adorned on royalty. As
the carriage drove away, she noticed a star shape cut out to make a
window in the back. She had a feeling she would see that carriage again.
          Willow couldn't help but wonder why such a carriage would be
going to Baxter. Baxter was a simple farming village. Yes, there were
some with means. But most people were simple men who worked the
land and women who cared for their children. The village people were like
a family. Strangers were not always welcomed into the village as those
believe it should be in a small God-fearing village. Strangers were
suspicious, until proven otherwise--a dangerous way of thinking.
Willow wondered how many of those villagers were hiding things.
Everyone hides things. People wear a mask, not to hide what they do not
want others to discover; but to hide what they fear most about themselves
and do not want to reveal. The peculiar thing about secrets is that they
are revealed when the time is right, no matter if we are prepared or not.

CHAPTER 12

Curiosity was getting the better of Willow even though she wasn't a person to pry. There was a sensation brewing that she couldn't ignore. She hadn't been in town for a couple of days. She knew if she didn't make an appearance soon rumors would sure to start. She let out a tiny giggle at that thought. Rumors were just results of an idle mind. In a small village, there were plenty of those.

She walked down her lane, taking in the fragrances of the day, and stopped when she reached the main road into town.

"Stand guard, my dear ones," she instructed as she patted the heads of two gargoyles who stood watch over her property.

She walked into town. Willow loved the entrance to the town. A cemetery was the first sight one sees when coming into the town from the west. Many would find the sight of grey stones a depressing sight instead of a welcoming sight. She thought the stones were a celebration of life! A celebration of God's many beautiful creations! For there to be life to anything there, must be death. The stones were a reminder of that cycle. She found the cemetery calming to her mind and soul. She smiled when she saw the peaks of the monuments.

"Blessed are those who rest in this hallowed ground. May your spirits not be bound," she whispered as she passed by the cemetery.

The Main Street of the village was quite simple. She loved walking under the tree-lined dirt road. Willow smiled at the thought of the beauty those trees would bring to the people of the town in the future. The fresh leaves of spring, the full shade of summer, and the changing colors of a fall masterpiece, before shedding their leaves in the cold winter.

A few houses occupied the street. Many of the homes were small and modest like her own. There was one house which stood out from all the other modest homes in the village. This dwelling would not be classified as modest at all. It was a gigantic house compared to the others. But it would not be classified as majestic due to those occupied the house.

The house was a two-story home made of limestone and many other types of stones brought in from neighboring villages. The house had large grand windows facing the road. There was a stairway leading from the walkway to the house. The upstairs had rounded windows where one could see birds made their nests at one time, but not now. The trees around the house were dying, the roses were full of thorns and seemed to be trying to make their escape by climbing up the pillars on the front porch. One might think their colors of the roses were crying or bleeding because they could not escape their fate. The house could easily have been a grand house if the right person owned it. But the chance of circumstances changing were not in the cards anytime soon. However, one day the house would thrive as it was meant to and the roses would not be crying tears of sorrow but of joy.

The chimneys of the other houses were exhaling smoke to show they were busy at work. The windows were open to allow the fragrances from the flowers growing in the pots to envelop the homes with nature. The birds were happily singing their songs to add music to the playing children's laughter.

As you entered the street from the west, there was a church. It was a small white schoolhouse with a simple wooden door. It had a cast iron door handle made by the local blacksmith especially for the school. Willow heard the sound of the church bell ringing, which had also been made by the blacksmith. The ringing of the bell signaled it was noon to the townspeople. However, Willow could tell it was noon by the heat of the sun, which was in its full glory on this beautiful day.

On the east end of the street was a brick building. One might just walk by if they didn't know it was a business. It smelled of body odor, cigars, tobacco, and whiskey. Many of the men were in need of a good bath. The floor of the tavern, a combination of manure and dirt, added to the foul odor and brought many flies in for a free meal and shelter. It was the town's tavern, The Grumpy Bulldog. Willow had been in the tavern a few times. She couldn't stay in there long because the stench made her eyes and lungs ache. There were a few horses tied to the wooden rail outside the tavern. She looked for the carriage, but it was nowhere to be found.

Willow didn't realize how parched she was until that moment. She needed a drink to quench her urgent thirst. She knew the walk back to her house would be long. She could stop by Bethany Creek for a drink of the fresh cold creek water, but an ale sounded better than water.

Willow started towards the tavern with vigor and did not look back. She knew entering the tavern alone would cause a stir. Once the toe of her slipper entered the threshold of the tavern, the rumor mill would be grinding harder than Thatcher's Mill. She didn't care one bit about what people would say. She was thirsty and she had money to pay for her ale.

The whole tavern automatically turned to see who was entering the doors. The noise in the establishment turned deathly quiet. All eyes were on her as she stepped further into the smelly tavern. She could feel eyes of surprise, lust, anger, and even superiority on her as she continued to venture into what clearly was deemed a man's domain.

"You must be mistaken or lost. The ladies are meetin' at the church," a man stood up to inform her.

"Thank you, Mr. Wells, for your concern, but I am at the correct establishment," she confronted the man, then turned and spoke to the barman. "I am thirsty, and I would like an ale please."

"I don't think you understand. Look around. Do you see any other women in this tavern? No, because they know their place is not here. I would advise you to take their lead and do the same."

"Mr. Wells, I don't think you understand. I want a drink. I have the money to pay for it. So, I intend to enjoy an ale," she advised in a firm voice.

"Maybe you need to be escorted home!" Mr. Wells demanded as he forcefully took ahold of her arm.

"Unhand the woman at once!" A male voice boomed through the small tavern.

"Please, sir, give me your name? Do you know this woman?" Mr. Wells shouted still holding her arm and squeezing harder.

"My name and association are none of your business," the man retorted back with a hint of anger brewing in his voice.

"You are not from here. It is only polite and proper to state your name!"

"You are going to lecture me about being proper when you are the man who has a hold of a woman's arm to the point where her skin is turning white? You speak to this woman as if she is a farm animal! Now tell me, who is not being polite, let alone a gentleman. If you ask me, you are the one acting like a simple ass."

The stranger hit a nerve with Mr. Wells. Mr. Wells quickly released Willow's arm from his tight grip. One could see where he had held her arm so tight there were white marks where his fingers had been. She took her hand and rubbed the circulation back into her arm.

"I believe she ordered an ale. Please make it three and put it on his tab," the stranger said to the barman as he pointed to Mr. Wells. He then guided Willow to a table.

The tavern's atmosphere was still quiet and seemed to have a blanket of fear. Everyone was waiting to see what Mr. Wells' reaction was going to be to the stranger and to Willow. Mr. Wells had never been talked to in that manner from a stranger or a woman. He was known for his money and his temper, both of which could be a bad combination.

"Thank you, sir," Willow said as they sat down at a table.

"Are you okay? Maybe you need ice for your arm."

"I will be fine."

"I am sorry he treated you in the manner he thought he needed to treat you. Who in the hell is he anyway?"

"Amos Wells. He has money and a temper to boot. He is very used to getting what he wants when he wants it. No one has dared to challenge him. No one has stood up to him, at least not until today." The bartender explained as he brought over more ale for the two.

"Well, he should know how to treat a lady."

"Well, my kind sir, my stepping foot in this establishment denounces me as ever being a lady in the minds of many," Willow stated.

"I disagree and will gladly tell any man."

"I know you denied Amos the knowledge of your name, but may I have the privilege of knowing your name?"

"Only if I learn yours in return," he bargained.

"Fair enough," she agreed with a smile.

"My name is Liam Harper. It is nice to meet you," he introduced himself and extended his hand.

"Willow Oakes, it is nice to meet you as well," she replied as she shook his hand.

"Well, Ms. Oakes, please let me walk you home."

"Thank you, Mr. Harper. The walk to my cottage is long. I would not want you to being walking back here alone in the dark hour without a lantern."

"I have no concerns."

"Again, I appreciate the offer, but I will decline, for I would like to be alone with my thoughts. Thank you again for saving me from Mr. Wells's grip," she thanked him as she rose from her chair.

"May I at least walk you to the street?" he questioned.

"That is a fair compromise," she nodded.

The two walked to the door. She could feel all eyes on her once again. The feelings of anger, contempt, and admiration could be felt this time. She was not afraid. She felt words were not being said to her at this moment that people desperately wanted to say to her. Those words would come later. Mr. Wells was left in a corner drinking alone. The image of him alone needed no words.

"Thank you again for saving me. Good night, Mr. Harper," she said to Liam.

"If it is fate, we will," Liam responded.

Willow turned and began the long walk towards home.

Liam whispered under his breath, "I don't think you are the one who will need saving," as he walked to the back of the building and got into his carriage. He smiled at the sight of the shadow of a star in the seat across from him.

CHAPTER 13

Willow's trip into town was one memory that would not soon escape her mind. She smiled when she thought of Mr. Harper. He was a gentleman. She hoped the men took notice of how he stood up to Amos Wells!

The thought of that horrible man made her stomach turn a little sour. How could one person be so miserable? How could he be so mean to everyone? Why were people so intimidated by him? She took a look down at her arm. A tinge of purple color was starting to form in the shape of his fingers. It was at that moment Willow decided Amos Wells was not going to intimidate her anymore.

Willow loved walking right before the sun decided to retire. The walk home tonight was beautiful.   The colors of red, orange, yellow and sometimes purple made her automatically smile with pleasure. Nature was really the best artist there will ever be. People should treasure it more. She closed her eyes to remember the masterpiece perfectly in her mind.

Her happy thoughts were interrupted by the fierce growling of her stomach. She didn't realize she hadn't eaten anything all day long. Her stomach was alerting her the couple cups of tea this morning and the mug of ale earlier were not enough to satisfy it. It wanted real food. She rushed home in anticipation of a good meal. She wasn't going to let the sourness of Amos Wells ruin her day or her mood. After all, for every bit of darkness there is a light.   Liam Harper was the light in her day.

She was at her front door before she knew it. She looked up and saw the first stars begin to twinkle in the night sky. She smiled and went inside to fix and enjoy a good meal.

Willow thought about Mr. Liam Harper the whole evening. She dressed for bed and slept well that night with no dreams or disturbances to bother her slumber.

The next morning, she was awakened by a light knocking on her door.

"Willow! Willow! Open the door!" A woman wailed on the other side of the wooden door. Willow quickly grabbed her robe and rushed to answer the door.

"Just one moment, please," she said through the door as she unlocked the two bolts on the door.

"Willow, oh Willow! I need your help!" the woman gasped as Willow opened the door.

"Mary, calm down. Come inside and take a seat," Willow demanded before getting her morning visitor a cup of water.

"Thank you," Mary sobbed as she drank the water.

"Mary, you look a fright. What is the matter? What has you so upset?"

"Willow, it's my Henry."

"Henry? What about Henry?" Willow asked concerned for the woman sitting across from her.

"You need to come with me! You need to see for yourself!" Mary said with extreme agitation.

"Hold on. I'm not even dressed for the day. I am going to make you some tea."

"We don't have time for tea! We must hurry! We must go now!"

"Mary, my dear Mary, you need to try to stay calm. Drink this tea and I will get dressed. After I dress, we will see how we can help your Henry," she instructed as she prepared the tea.

Willow left the room to get dressed. She could see Mary from the doorway. Mary sat in the chair wringing her hands as if she was trying to wipe them clean of something. She could see Mary's lips moving as if in silent prayer. She couldn't determine what words she was saying. She was not a lip reader.

Willow hurried to dress. She did not want to leave her friend alone for very long. Mary was very distraught. Willow was genuinely concerned for her friend's state of mind. She had known Mary for many years. They had become quick friends. Mary was older than Willow by about five years. Mary had been through a lot emotionally lately. It was clear by Mary's appearance and tone of voice she was lacking sleep. Willow knew she had to help her. But she wondered if her help was going to be enough to calm her dear friend.

The tea kettle screamed for attention, taking Willow out of her thoughts, and making her hurry even more. She rushed to the stove to cease the kettle's screams. Quickly she made two cups of tea and served one to her friend.

"Here, Mary. Take a good drink of the tea. Don't worry about the temperature. It will not burn your mouth," Willow instructed as she handed her the cup of steaming liquid.

Mary gave her hostess a doubting look. Willow nodded then took a drink of her own hot liquid. Mary did as she was instructed. The tea did seem to calm her. She stopped wringing her hands. Her breath calmed so she could talk normally.

"Now, tell me about Henry," Willow asked.

"He came to visit me yesterday!"

"Yesterday?"

"Yes, and again before I came here," Mary said, shaking her head up and down.

"I see how his visit upset you. Do you want me to go speak with him?"

"Oh, Willow! I don't want to make him angry," Mary exclaimed, shaking her head. She took another sip of tea.

"Have you asked him not to visit you?"

"No. What if I want him to come back?" she said, starting to panic again.

"I will go and talk to him today. I will ask him to leave you alone for a bit of time. Take this pouch of tea. This will calm your nerves and help you sleep," she said as she handed Mary a yellow pouch of tea.

"Oh Willow. What have I done to deserve this torment?"

"Mary, you are not at fault at all. Henry is just lost. You will have peace soon," Willow comforted her friend.

"Thank you! Thank you so much!"

"You are most welcome. Now, let's talk about something more pleasant, shall we?" she smiled at her friend.

"I wish I could. I feel terrible for not staying. But I need to go home and collect the eggs from the chickens."

"Another time. We will share a piece of pie. Rest assured Henry and I will have a conversation."

"Thank you so much. You are a great friend. May the Lord bless you always," Mary gushed as she hugged her.

"May the Lord bless your home also."

Willow assisted Mary out the door and shut it behind her. She started to clean her table immediately. While Mary was there, she hadn't noticed her arm was now showing her encounter with Amos was a deep, deep purple. She felt herself become angry. She released the anger almost immediately because she wanted a clear mind when she had her conversation with Henry.

Willow gathered the necessary things she needed to talk to Henry. She was not fearful of the upcoming encounter she was about to have with Henry. She relaxed the rest of the day, not overdoing the needed tasks. She decided to wait until the light of the moon was visible but not enough for anyone to see her. She found her black cloak and left to see Henry.

The nightlife was singing its nocturnal songs. She loved the night so much more than the day. The world was different in the moonlight. The world was a slower pace in the light of the moon versus the heat of the sun. The sun was a fiery reminder that one must hurry to accomplish what needed to be done before it decided to extinguish its light leaving the people stressed and uneasy.

The night doesn't put any pressure on anyone. The moon provided no heat to pressure you to do anything. The animals did their own thing without any worries. She was happiest in the light of the moon. She welcomed the cooler weather, a twenty-degree difference from the heat of the sun.

She stopped to say hello to her faithful guardians.

"It is a great night. The clouds are hiding the moonlight tonight. Be careful, dear ones. Fly carefully," she said and touched their wings.

She couldn't remember where she had gotten her faithful friends. They had been part of her house for as long as she could remember. They had been with her through everything. People would look at them and see these ugly creatures made of stone. But to her, they were her friends, her protectors. The mere thought of the two statues made her smile. The caw of a crow brought her thoughts back to the task at hand, Henry.

She continued to walk until she finally reached her destination. The moonlight was covered by clouds. The trees had not shed their leaves making her almost invisible to anyone.

"Henry, it's me, Willow," she began.

Silence.

"I have come to talk to you."

Silence.

"Mary came to see me today. You need to stop visiting her. She doesn't want you to come for a while. Please understand."

Silence.

Willow sat on the ground in silence for a couple of minutes listening to the crickets and frogs having their nightly conversations.

"Henry, I am going to go now. Please be nice and come to talk to me when you need to talk." Willow stood up to go.

She started to walk away only to stop to see what the moon was revealing to her:

> Henry Marx
> Son of George and Mary
> Died at 7 years, 3 months, 17 days

"Rest in peace, little Henry," whispered Willow.

"Moon so bright, shine its light. Protect all who fell a fright. Keep us safe from harms' way, let not even get its way," she chanted to the night air and the moon.

She didn't know why she felt uneasy. She felt something was not right. She felt eyes on her that didn't belong to any nocturnal animal of the night.

"Who's there?" Willow asked as she looked around at her surroundings.

Silence.

She could feel the eyes watching her with an intensity fiercer than anything she had ever felt in all her years. Her whole body became tense. She could feel a burning sensation in her body.

"I know you are there! Show yourself!" She demanded into the night air.

The night music was silent as if to listen to whatever was going to happen next. The atmosphere was heavy. One could feel a blanket of fear and anger replacing the happy and carefree air which was present only minutes before. The clouds covered the moon as a blindfold so it wouldn't witness the events that were about to take place.

Willow stood as still as a statue to listen intently to the night. She didn't see or hear anything. Willow decided to go forward towards her home. She was not going to let this frighten her anymore.

"You may shine your light again, dear moon. Your light is much needed and appreciated," she asked of the moon.

The clouds instantly parted and, in doing so, illuminated the meadow in front of her. In the meadow, she saw a figure. It was too far away to determine if it was a man or a woman. She did see a beautiful owl flying in the meadow. She followed the bird with her eyes. When she looked back at the meadow again, the figure was gone. She walked a little further until she reached her gate. The sight of her stone friends gave her extreme relief. It was only then that she didn't feel the eyes upon her. She felt safe.

CHAPTER 14

Willow's continued thoughts and feelings of being watched did not allow her much sleep. She had never felt like that before in the night hours. The night was her comfort zone. She usually was one with the night. She was perplexed at how she was uneasy she was feeling tonight.

She rose from her bed and decided to start her day early. She wanted to go to the meadow to pick some plants and flowers. She wanted to see if the figure from the dream left anything behind. Willow made a cup of tea and listened to the last of the frogs and crickets' duet.

She closed her eyes to take in the music. The lightly blowing wind felt good to her. It was Mother Nature's breath of fresh air. The wind was teasing her hair causing it to brush on her face. She felt at peace for the moment.

The last few days had been very tiring on the mind, body, and soul. She woke up on the floor, looking as if she had been caught in a storm. Her body was still sending her reminders of the hard floor by her aching muscles. The encounter with Amos Wells, still fresh in her memory. Only a tiny bit of the finger imprints remained. Finally, the events of the previous night of the peering eyes and the figure of the meadow still haunted her. What could they all mean?

"May the unseen be seen," she said as she closed her eyes.

Willow left her home after she finished her tea and walked to the meadow. The sun wasn't up yet. The fragrance of the early meadow filled her nose. She looked around for a clue of the observer from the night before but found nothing. There wasn't even a flattened spot to even show where a person would have been standing. No footprints to show a path taken in or out of the meadow. Maybe she had imagined seeing the person. She had a difficult time comprehending the notion because her eyesight and senses were always spot on. Her mind was tired, she concluded.

She knew her head would definitely begin to hurt if she kept those questions in her mind. Willow decided to put the thoughts and questions out of her mind about the night before and went to the forest to pick wild raspberries.

The forest was beautiful in the morning light. Yes, Willow loved the night. The night calmed her in the way the morning never could. But the morning light coming through the open spaces in the leaves cast the perfect shadows for the flowers to dance to the wind in perfect harmony. The umbrella of the tree leaves made the weather perfect berry picking weather. She took her basket and started to pick the ripe berries, stopping to eat a few every now and then to give her tongue a sweet treat. The raspberries tasted sweet on her tongue. And it would even have a sweeter taste when they were made into a pie.

While picking berries, she heard a faint chirping in the grass. She looked around and found a tiny bird who must have fallen to the ground when he was trying learn to fly.

"Hold on little one." She picked up and caressed the bird lightly.

The bird sat calmly in her hand, not frightened at all by the human who was holding him in her gentle hand.

"There, there. I know it hurts, doesn't it? Don't be scared. I'll make it better," she cooed, stroking his head.

The other birds were curious, wondering was happening to their feathered friend. The birds were chirping quietly now, as if they were comforting their friend. Willow caressed the bird from head to tail. She looked into the bird's eyes, blew it a kiss and gently let it perch on her arm.

"Come on, you can do it. Go ahead. Join your friends," she encouraged her feathered friend.

The tiny bird took little hops until it finally reached a point where it could take off into flight. The little bird took off and flew as if nothing had happened to him. Willow smiled with satisfaction.

"Aren't you sweet?" a gruff voice asked smugly, making her turn around on her heels.

"What are you doing here? You should have made your presence known. You startled me," she said, catching her balance from turning so quickly.

"I thought nothing scared the great Willow Oakes," the man said, unmounting from his horse.

"I didn't say I was scared. I said I was startled. There is a difference," she informed him, standing her ground.

"Is there really a difference?"

"Mr. Wells, I am not scared of you," she said, automatically grabbing her arm where he had left bruises on her arm before.

His gaze went to her arm. He had a certain satisfaction of seeing those bruises on her arm. The bruises were confirmation of his power and the fear that he instills in people. The thought of that fear and power made him smile as if he were the Devil himself.

"Willow, you should be scared of me," Amos retorted as he walked closer to her.

"Why should I be scared of you?"

"I can make your life miserable, or I can make it great. I have money. I have power," he boasted.

"Mr. Wells, the only thing that you have is a heart full of greed."

"Actually, I was looking for you." Amos Wells replied, changing the subject.

"Looking for me? Why?"

"I wanted to give you a chance to apologize to me for the other night at the tavern."

Willow laughed aloud at his suggestion. He really was conceited and possibly out of his mind.

"Mr. Wells, I will not apologize to you. That is one thing you will not get from me," she scoffed and turned to walk away.

"Woman! Where in the hell do you think you are going!" he boomed and rushed to grab her arm.

"Let go of me!" she demanded, pulling her arm and trying to get away.

"Not this time! I always get what I want. You made a fool out of me! You and that stranger. I can't find him. But I found you. You are going to learn some respect. And you are going to learn your place!" He ranted as he grabbed and pushed her against a tree. Willow hit the tree so hard that loose tree limbs fell to the ground from the impact. The tree bark made tiny cuts on the back of her neck, arms and legs.

"Mr. Wells, let me go!" she hissed.

"I'm not done with you! I always get what I want. I want you!" he sneered as he ripped open the front of her dress, exposing a portion of her breast.

He placed one hand on her mouth, and another traveled under her skirt. His eyes maintained his constant stare into hers and looked like the devils'. She closed her eyes briefly to break that gaze. She knew she had to stop him. She could feel her anger boiling like water in a tea kettle.

Willow allowed her body to go slightly limp in the hope he would loosen his grip. She kissed him, then kissed him again. He still maintained a grip on her arm. She finally noticed his tongue enter her mouth. When she felt his tongue on the edge of her teeth, she clamped down and bit as hard as she could. The taste of blood filled her mouth like a small river overflowing after a heavy rain.

"You bitch!" Amos yelled as he grabbed his mouth with his hand.

She looked at him only for a brief second before mounting his horse in a single jump and galloped as fast as the animal's legs would take them. Willow did not look back once she was on the horse. Her heart was beating as fast as the mount was galloping. The horse must have sensed the two were out of Amos's sight. He slowed down so they could catch their breath, and their bearings. Willow knew where she was. She knew she couldn't be seen with Amos's horse. He would definitely accuse her of stealing.

"Thank you, friend. Go find Amos. For if you don't, the next time I ride you, it will be to my hanging," she told the animal. She dismounted the beast and watched it trot off to find Amos.

She looked around at the surroundings to find a sense of calm. She could still taste Amos's blood in her mouth. With the rush of getting away, she didn't realize she had been holding her breath. The vile liquid was still in her mouth. She spit out the crimson liquid as soon as she realized she needed to breathe and to be free of the wretched taste. She let out her breath, and with that breath, vomit came out like a rush of crows once they spot a dead animal in the middle of a field.

"Home," she thought and started to cry uncontrollably.

Her body fell upon the ground in a deep, emotional exhaustion. She wanted to just sleep. She knew she couldn't stay there no matter how badly she wanted to just lie there and let all the emotions drain out of her until there was nothing left. She closed her eyes and let out a sob. When she opened her eyes again, she was in her bed. She immediately returned to a deep sleep.

Willow woke up with a jolt as if she were struck by lightning. The memory of the previous event returned to her and she was angry as a hornet. She looked at her dress and traced the rip with her hands. She looked at her arm and fresh bruises were present with more intensity. She looked at herself in the looking glass and saw dried blood around her lips. She still could taste his blood! The sight and taste of Amos's blood gave her an undescribed energy she couldn't put into words. She knew what she had to do. The great design was being put into motion, unbeknownst to everyone, including Willow.

CHAPTER 15

The smell of smoke filling her nose woke Willow from her sleep. She looked out the window to discover a fire blazing. Her garden was enveloped in a fiery ring of orange and red. She rushed out of the house, still in her bedclothes. Her feet paid no heed to the rocks in her driveway. She looked about to see the fire angrily spreading at a rapid rate. The flames were widening its circle faster than her eyes could follow.

"*Ingris Lucius Annaeus Senca!*" She yelled at the fire with as much force as the fire contained.

"In this fire and of the flame, send it back to where it came!" she chanted as a ball of fire appeared in her hand and the garden fire disappeared.

The fireball floated about a half an inch above her hand. She was exempt from the fire's heat. She let it dance for a minute or two. As she stared into the dancing flames of the ball, her anger started to grow. The colors of yellow, orange and red became more intense as her anger grew.

"Go, travel and find your way. Disclose who started this fire another day. May the person who started the flame. Everyone will know who is to blame." She said as the fireball disappeared into the night sky.

Willow went to the circle where the ring of fire left its imprint, grabbed two handfuls of dirt and ash, blew one handful into the direction of town and placed the other in her pocket. She turned promptly on one heel, went back inside, and fell back to sleep knowing the Universe was at work.

Willow awoke from the best sleep she had in many moons. She needed to make a trip into town. She hoped she would see Mary to ask her about Henry. She had not seen or talked to her friend since her visit. She dressed quickly and made her way to town.

The town was alive with the chatter of the townspeople when Willow arrived in town. There was excitement in the air. Willow could feel it in her bones. Their eyes were wide and tongues were busy. She had a challenging time walking down the street, not due to the ruts on the road made by carriages when it rains, but by the crowd of people.

"What brings everyone out so early?"

"The light in the sky last night. Did you see it?" Mary asked in awe.

"No, I retired early."

"It was as if fire was in the sky. A huge fireball fell to the earth from the sky! What could it mean?"

"Maybe it was an omen of a fallen soul. Maybe someone's soul is in danger. Or a soul has been released from Hell," Willow explained.

"Everyone to the church for a meeting!" someone yelled above the crowd.

"We better get going." Willow smiled at Mary and they started their way to the little church.

The white church stood at the opposite end of Main Street. The Grumpy Bulldog and the church squaring off, each holding their ground on opposite ends of the street. The ironic thing about the placement of the two buildings was a perfect representation of the battle of Heaven and Hell in living color. Many times, it depended on the day of the week to determine which building was Heaven and which was Hell.

The events in the tavern on a Saturday night definitely would be Heaven for anyone who was in the establishment. Some patrons were simply there for a beverage just like she. Others were there for the spirits to drown their problems. Satan and his minions don't have to work so hard with the willing.

The people who relish in the heaven of the Grumpy Bulldog's spirits and atmosphere no doubt sit in a hard pew in God's house exchanging looks with those same people who they shared a drink with just a few hours before. Willow didn't judge or condemn those people. It was not her place or her job. That was up to God.

The church had seven wooden steps, with a wood railing that had a design of manger on one side with intricate carvings of the angel, star, Mary, Joseph, and baby Jesus in the stable. The carving on the entry side of the railing reminded the people of the birth of Christ, the Messiah, who's birth was foretold. The exit side of the church was the three crosses of the crucifixion on the hill of Golgotha. Three figures of men, one more detailed than the other two crosses. It was a reminder to the people exiting the church that Jesus died for their sins.

The doors were solid black walnut. The doors each had six panels. The top of the doors peaked like an arch. The handles of the doors were iron along with all the hardware. The doors were heavy to open. Most of the time, the doors were left open due to their heaviness.

The steeple was directly above the grand doors. The steeple welcomed everyone with its bell which was made when the church was built. The lantern was brought with the founders of the village church. Legend has it that the lantern was almost out of oil until the founders stepped on that very spot when the light of the lantern shone bright. And the rest is history. The lantern is only lit on three days: the day the town was founded, February 16th, Christmas at midnight; and Easter morning at sunrise. The light of the lantern blankets the town perfectly in all directions. Willow loved the days when the lantern's light shone on the town. She loved her town. Even though she didn't live directly in town, her heart was clearly bound to the town.

The bell was made by the local blacksmith shortly after the church was constructed. The church was the first building constructed, after some small houses. The bell was rung at seven in the morning, to let everyone know their day should be beginning soon, noon to let people know to take a break, and to inform people of the start of church. People knew if the church bell was ringing at other times, it warranted their attention.

Once inside the grand doors, a raw wooden cross was placed on the altar beneath three rectangle windows. The windows held the words peace, joy and love. The altar was made from the same wood as the railings and doors. The altar had the carving of the tree of life with two other trees in the background. A carved inscription encompassed the tree with the words "To Thine Own Self Be True." Willow was always drawn to the pulpit. The bible of Mr. Sidney, the official founder, was always on the pulpit. A cross carved of wood with a climbing olive branch was just big enough to be noticed but not to distract the church members from the sermons.

There were three arched windows on each side of the church to let the sunshine and fresh air into the building. When the sun caused shadows, the six windows all met in the middle to form a perfect picture. There were shutters that could be closed would shield the windows from the elements or prevent anyone from peering inside the church itself.

On each side of the church floor were six five-foot long, beautiful cherry wood pews. Bibles and song books were waiting to be picked up and used. The polished pews shone brightly in the natural light.

The stove was silent due to the warm weather. It had earned a well-deserved rest while waiting to be called into use. When the weather required it, the aroma of pine or cedar filled the air of the church.

There were nine candle lanterns holding three candles suspended from the wooden beams on the ceiling. The light from the candles reflected off the glass in the lanterns, constructing the mood of serenity, calmness and peace.

Many people were already seated in the pews when Willow entered the church. She smiled when she entered. She and Mary found a place to sit in the middle of the church.

Willow looked around the church. It was filling up fast. Those who entered wore a consistent look for fear. Some tried to pretend everything was okay with them, but their eyes told a different story.

Willow's eyes were drawn to the lanterns. The two outside candles were burning at a slow steady pace. The middle candle's flame was fluctuating between a high then low dance. She gazed out the window and noticed the sun and clouds were playing a friendly game of hide and seek. The way the game made the shadows dance was incredible.

"May I have your attention please!" Pastor Davis announced from the pulpit.

The church went from chatter to silence in the matter of seconds. The flames even quit doing their dance to a little sway. The Pastor had their full attention. They were eager to hear what he had to say.

"My good people, we have witnessed a strange phenomenon last night," the Pastor began.

"Wait, Sir Amos Wells is not present. Should we wait?" a man from the back pew asked.

"Mr. Wells can hear the church bells ringing just like we all did. There is no reason to waste everyone's time because he cannot manage his own," Mr. Holl commented as many others shook their heads in agreement.

Willow sat silently in her pew. This was one thing Amos Wells was not going to be able to control. She did find it odd that Amos was not present in the church to flaunt his self-proposed authority. There was not a subject Amos did not know about--not one. His blessing was intelligence, and his curse was no common sense; but his deadly sin was arrogance. Lucifer was arrogant and all know how that turned out.

"There are plenty of us here who can relay the happenings here today."

"We are not here to discuss Amos Wells. We are here to discuss what we all saw in the night sky last night," Mr. Holl expressed.

"Okay. We all saw a strange event in the sky last night. I want to assure you there is nothing to worry about. No one was hurt in the event, no livestock killed, and no real property damage that we are aware," Pastor Davis stated.

"Does anyone know where the fireball landed?"

"No, I assume it just dissolved," Pastor Davis said.

"Did the Good Lord send us a sign of plague to come as in Biblical times? Is this the beginning of the Rapture?" Old Widow Long questioned in a panicked voice causing a few murmurs in the church.

"Mrs. Long, I'm sure this is not a plague God is ascending upon us," Pastor Davis assured in a calm voice.

"Willow did say it could be an omen or a fallen soul released from Hell," Mary blurted out, then covered her mouth with her hand as to trap any further words which may escape inside.

Mary might as well say Willow had a conversation with the Devil himself. The congregation of people started to mumble softly at first, then voices started to rise. Willow could feel eyes on her from every direction. She knew she had to say something to calm the people's worries which were just heightened by Mary's words.

"May I?" Willow asked as she started to walk to the pulpit.

"Of course, please," Pastor Davis said with a welcoming gesture.

Willow walked up to the pulpit, took a deep breath, and looked out at all the people. The voices were hushed and the church was quiet waiting for her words.

"Dear Friends, I did tell Mary that it could be a fallen soul escaping from Hell. Let me be clear--that is a superstition. Friends, I don't believe that God is sending a plague or it's a bad omen. I believe we should think of it as a good sign from the heavens. Why must every unexplainable thing be bad?" she asked, looking at the group in the church.

Not a word was uttered. The church was silent. One couldn't even hear people in the pews breathing. Blank stares were all she was receiving while she was standing there waiting for someone to speak.

"I think Willow makes a good point. She has brought to our attention to something not a one of us or had thought maybe a possibility," a man finally broke the silence.

"Pastor Davis, what do you think?" Willow asked knowing his answer would either bring chaos or calmness to the church.

Pastor paused, then he joined her at the pulpit. He looked at Willow in the eyes before he started to speak.

"My Friends, I believe our sister Willow is correct. Satan has tricked our minds to think He is behind the fireball in the sky we all witnessed. Dear friends, we should be ashamed of ourselves! Isn't God who created the skies? Isn't God who created Hell? Isn't God who banished Lucifer to the fiery pit of Hell? We need to be asking ourselves this question: why would a God, our God who created the stars, moon and the beauty of the night sky allow Satan to invade it? We should ask God for forgiveness for assuming this was Satan's work. We need to tell Satan he is not welcomed in our homes, community or minds!" Pastor Davis's voice echoed throughout the church.

Willow, still standing beside the pastor both looking out on the congregation who was frightened and uncertain not five minutes before, now had a look of comfort, joy, and relief.

"Thank you, Pastor Davis, for those words. Dear friends, we need to perceive the event of last night as a blessing of things to come for our little community. God is good!" Mr. Holl exclaimed with excitement.

"God is good!" a few repeated back to Mr. Holl.

"Brad is correct, let's go forth and be excited about what the Good Lord has planned for each and every one of us, today and tomorrow!" Pastor said with a smile.

"This is the day that the Lord has made! Let us rejoice and be glad in it! Enjoy today and every day of our lives to come!" Bradley said standing up.

The church meeting turned into a mini celebration. The joyful looks on the people's faces made Willow happy. She stepped down from the pulpit and went back to her pew.

"Friends, have a blessed rest of your week, until we meet again on Sunday. Go in peace and love," Pastor Davis concluded before stepping down from the pulpit.

The people stayed and chit chatted amongst each other for some time. Willow exchanged pleasantries and quietly slipped out of the church without anyone noticing. She smiled with relief and gratitude when the fresh air and sunshine was felt by her body. God was truly showing His masterpiece on this day. She stood in the street marveling at the little village and everything around her. When a butterfly matching the colors God was using for this palette of colors landed on her arm.

"Well, aren't you a beautiful creature?" she asked the pink, blue, and royal shade of lavender as it stayed perched on her arm. The winged creature expanded its wings on the bruises of Willow's reminder of her two encounters with Amos Wells. The bruises were so detailed. If one would examine the marking close enough, they would see the fingerprints and a space on a finger where a ring was present. The wings of the butterfly wrapped around the bruises as if it were caressing it with comfort.

Willow lightly caressed the wings, praying she wouldn't scare it away. The creature let her stroke its wings as if she were petting a cat or dog. The wings only fluttered a couple of times to let Willow know it trusted her.

"Aren't you special? Don't be afraid I won't hurt you," she said with calmness.

The butterfly fully expanded its wings as if it were resting for just a bit. Willow and her new winged friend were in their own time and space. She didn't notice or hear the town resuming the normal activities after the meeting at the church.

"Thank goodness I found you, Willow!" Mary rushed forward and touched her arm, breaking Willow's trance. Willow pulled back as if Mary's touch were as hot as a blacksmith's hot iron.

"Hello, Mary."

"I am asking for your forgiveness. I should have kept your words to myself. Please, forgive me, my friend," Mary begged.

"There is nothing for you to ask my forgiveness, Mary. You didn't offend me in any matter," Willow said as she gave her friend a reassuring smile.

"You are too kind! Many of the other women would be ready to disown me as a friend."

"Mary, as we both know, I'm not like most women. Do not worry any longer."

"You speak the truth. You are not like any other woman I know or shall know. May the Lord shed many blessings on you," Mary said as she hugged Willow.

"You also," Willow said returning the gesture.

"I must be going. Bertie will be restless if I don't milk her soon," Mary said as she walked away.

"God is good," Pastor Davis said as he stood beside Willow.

"That He is." Willow agreed.

"I heard you make a rather good cherry jam.'

"Satisfactory I suppose."

"I would like to purchase a jar."

"Pastor, come by later tonight and you will have fresh baked bread with your jam."

"Perfect."

"I better be going. The bread won't bake itself," Willow said cheerfully before making her journey home after a very eventful trip to town.

CHAPTER 16

Willow started making the bread as soon as she arrived home. She found kneading of the dough very relaxing, almost therapeutic. The dough between her fingers reminded her of the mud between her feet when it would rain. She placed the ball of dough in a bowl. Willow moved a stone she had set near the fireplace to warm earlier to the table where she placed the bowl of dough to rise and covered it with a towel.

Willow decided to check the cherries on the trees and pick more for jam or pies in the coming days. The air had cooled some from when she walked home from the church. Her cottage was going to get hot from the bread baking. She relished the cooler air now while available. She left her door open to allow the air to drift in to cool the house.

Willow grabbed her wooden bowl and set off to pick some bright, ripe red cherries. The cherry trees were just beyond the gates of her house. She had nurtured those trees from saplings. There were many times she thought they were about going to die, but a little encouragement went a long way. Now the trees were tall and thriving.

She went to one of the fruit trees and shook the limbs just enough for a few dozen cherries to fall, providing the animals a small snack. She was intruding on their homestead and taking their food. Providing the furry and feathered friends some food was only the courteous thing to do.

After some of the animals helped themselves, she began to pick the cherries. She took one and popped it in her mouth. The fruit tasted sweet with a tad bit of bitterness that lingered after she swallowed. These trees were as unique as the cherries. The fruit did not contain a horrible pit which reminded the eater to slow down when eating. When her wooden bowl was full, she sat down under the tree to enjoy the shade its leaves and branches provided. She couldn't help herself. She ate a half a dozen more cherries.

"I must stop before my stomach becomes angry," she said to a rabbit who hopped into her lap.

The rabbit was calm like a tame housecat that would be sitting in her lap. She carefully raised her hand to stroke the small forest animal. The creature with long ears and a fuzzy tail nested in her lap and sat there as if it were a natural thing for it to do. She placed a few cherries in her hand and let the animal nibble.

While sitting, she could hear the birds carrying on conversations with one another. The wind was making herself known when she felt appropriate. The sun was not going to be ignored either. The bright light beamed her rays through the clouds.

Willow closed her eyes and smiled at nature's friendly competition. She relished in the ray of sunshine finding her face and the warmth making it pink from its gentle heat.

Her mind traveled to the ring of fire that raged in her yard just hours before and the fireball in the sky. The image of Amos Wells' face came rushing into the forefront in her mind. She could almost smell the rancid odor of his breath. The memory of the stench made her stomach queasy. The thought of Amos Wells disgusted her to her very bone! He was a vile man. The rabbit nudged her hand bringing her out of her thoughts of Amos Wells.

"Hey little one, are they all gone?" she asked as she picked up the bunny and looked it in the eyes. The animal looked away to a batch of clover as if he wanted a bite of the plant. She gently put the animal on the ground and watched it enjoy the clover as much as the cherries.

She looked up at the sky and noticed darker clouds starting to make their presence known to the forest. The rumbling of thunder was not present but would be making itself known in due time. Rain was coming. She could smell it in the air. It was the feeling in her bones that caused her alarm. A succession of three echoing booms was enough of a warning for all to take cover from the impending storm about to happen. The animals took heed to the sky's warning. She knew she needed to follow suit.

She stood up, brushed off her dress, picked up her basket and started on her way back home. The venture home was not as leisurely as the walk to the forest. The animals were preparing themselves for the upcoming rain. She even found her steps were quicker with each boom of the thunder's constant warnings of what was to come. She prayed the rain would refrain from happening until after her visit with Pastor Davis.

Pastor Davis and Willow became instant friends. They had known one another for years. She adored the man of the cloth. She liked to believe the feeling was somewhat mutual. She enjoyed spending time with him. She always knew he would be honest with her and respect her even if she disagreed with him. He made her smile with his quick dry wit. She felt a tinge of guilt come across her for thinking about a Man of God in such a way different from him being a spiritual advisor. She couldn't help how she felt, and she would not apologize for it either.

She reached her lane and breathed a sigh of relief. She knew she was safe and wouldn't get wet coming home. She went to the loaves of bread at her table; they had risen very well while she was on her cherry-picking expedition. She placed the two loaves of bread in her stone oven and went to work on a small supper for her friend, Pastor Davis, and herself.

The skies were getting angrier by the minute. The winds were calm for the moment and had not yet made her entrance, like the belle of a southern barbeque in the Old South. Not to fret she would be making her entrance, just at the right time.

Willow stood on her porch and watched the gray storm clouds doing somersaults in the sky. The color of the clouds reminded her of the dandelion when the yellow has left and only the silvery gray of the flower remains, waiting and hoping someone would make a wish on it.

The clouds weren't as dark over the town as they were by her place. The cloud cover over the church was barely silver. The whole town was the same with one exception. The storm clouds over a particular residence were very ominous.

"Caw!" a crow made his presence known as he landed in front of her.

"Oh my! You scared me!"

"Caw! Caw!" he squawked again.

Willow looked up to find several crows flying in the sky. The flight was not a normal one for these birds. The black birds were usually ones that kept to themselves. Crows do not like to be bothered.

"You go tell your friend to hurry to shelter before the storm comes."

"Caw!" again the bird cried out, not leaving but instead moving closer.

"What are you trying to tell me? Do you have a message for me?" she asked the crow as she put her arm out so the bird could perch on her arm.

"Be careful, the claws are sharp. He could badly hurt you," Pastor Davis warned from the side of her.

"Pastor, I didn't see you there," she said embarrassed and watched the bird fly away.

"Willow, you can call me Christopher."

"What would people think?" she smiled and asked laughing.

"Since when have you cared about what people think?" he smiled and started to laugh.

"Never. Are you hungry?"

"Always."

"Sit please. Would you like something to drink?" she offered as they went inside.

"Whatever you are drinking will be perfect for me," he said as he sat down at the table.

Willow poured two glasses of water, made their plates and sat down at the table with her guest. She looked at her guest. He seemed pleased with the meal in front of him. There was ham, potatoes, corn, and fresh-baked bread with cherry jam. He grabbed his fork, ready to partake of the delicious meal.

"Aren't you going to pray?" Willow asked, making him stop in his tracks.

"Oh." he said embarrassed.

"That's okay. I will forgive you," she smiled before bowing her head.

"Dear Heavenly Father, thank you for this meal and the hands that have prepared it. Blessings to all. Amen."

"Amen," Willow thanked.

"So, tell me what you really think about the fireball and how did your arm heal so quickly." Christopher asked before taking a drink of his water.

Willow was caught off guard by his questions. They had been friends since they were children. She didn't understand why he was asking the questions.

"What do you mean?" Willow asked before taking a sip herself.

"Do you believe what you told the people in the church today?"

"I don't believe God is punishing us. I don't believe it's anything from God or Satan. I believe it was something for one person not for many." Willow explained to her religious friend.

"Someone in town?" Christopher asked.

"Maybe. Christopher, why the questions?"

"I heard you made Amos Wells quite angry when you visited The Grumpy Bulldog," he began.

"Yes, I was there and we had words," she confirmed.

"I heard he grabbed your arm quite tightly."

Willow's eyes traveled to her arm where the bruises of Amos's fingers were. Her mind traveled to when he attacked her in the forest.

"Yes, thankfully a kind stranger put him in his place."

"I can imagine how well Amos handled that situation." Christopher said before taking a bite.

"Not well."

"Is that how you got the bruises on your arm?"

"How I?" she stumbled to find words.

"Willow, I know things. I know more things than people realize. I need your help, Willow."

"My help? How can I help you?"

"Pour us more water and I will be glad to tell you.   Oh, and pass that cherry jam," he said with a smile like a child on Christmas morning.

CHAPTER 17

The two friends finished their meal and their conversation and Christopher headed home with jam in tow. Mother Nature was gracious enough to hold off with the storm until after Pastor left. The ride home from Willow's house was a quiet one of reflection for the Pastor. The reflection left him with mixed feelings, but most of all a feeling of hope. When Christopher closed the front door of his home, the skies resumed their fighting. Christopher took off his boots, put more wood on the fire, lit his pipe, listened to the weather outside and smiled knowing God was in control.

Christopher lit a candle, began to read this Bible and drank a cup of tea. The music Mother Nature was providing this night had a calming effect on him. When it rained, God was providing a way of cleaning everything to make it new again. Christopher felt change was coming. The storm of change would be bigger than the storm brewing outside. He knew whatever was coming, Willow would be able to handle.

Christopher woke up with a start the next morning. He had fallen asleep in his chair still in his clothes with his Bible neatly in his lap. The melody of the storm must have put him to sleep like a mother's lullaby does to a baby.

He opened his door to the brilliant sunrise. The colors of the sunrise were vibrant combination of violet, blue, orange, and red all complementing the green of the grass perfectly. Christopher smiled at God's creation.

"Joy truly does come in the morning," he thought as he went back inside his home to get ready for his day.

Pastor's dwelling was a modest one, truly designed with a bachelor in mind. Four rooms were all that made the house: kitchen, bedroom, living room, and a little storage room which he used as a prayer room.

There were windows in each room to allow natural light, two fireplaces--one in the bedroom and one in the living room--floors were made of wood and an outside provided a place for his horses and gardens. The home was quite plain when you compare it to the grand church beside the dwelling. God would provide was the philosophy of the builders of the house.

The size of the house never bothered him or was a concern until recently. He became the pastor of the church when he was just seventeen. The goals and mindset of the future of a seventeen-year-old man is quite different from an almost twenty-one-year-old man. Priorities change. Feelings changed. Things become clearer. God's plan becomes clearer.

Christopher decided he wanted a family. The house that the church provided was not a fitting place for that to happen. This dwelling was definitely for a lifelong bachelor. His thoughts wondered what life would be like to have a family. A beautiful, loving wife to raise good children. A good, faithful woman to share the blessings and trials God had in store for them as man and wife, a Godly couple. He could almost hear the laughter of his wife and children. Yes, that is what he wanted. A family would definitely be in his prayers beginning this day.

As he got dressed into some fresh, clean clothes, he found himself smiling. He made himself breakfast of eggs, ham, homemade bread with the most delicious cherry jam he had ever tasted. He said a little prayer of thanksgiving, took a bite of the delicious food and smiled as he thought of the person who prepared the jam. His peaceful thoughts were interrupted by a pounding on his door. The pounding crescendoing with each urgent pound.

"I'm coming!" he called out to the person on the other side of his door.

More urgent pounding.

"I'm coming!" he shouted again.

The pounding calmed a bit when the person heard the unlocking of the door.

"May I help you?" Christopher asked as he opened the door.

"I'm looking for the Pastor," a little woman said.

"I'm the Pastor. How may I help you?" he asked.

"I am here to ask for your help. Help for my daughter!" The woman said with desperation.

"What is wrong with your daughter?"

"She needs prayer. Satan is trying to invade her mind! I need a man of God to pray for her!"

"Dear Woman, I will pray for your daughter, and I will pray over your daughter, but I will not do an exorcism."

"Please, kind Sir, just a few drops of holy water upon her head is all I ask," the woman begged.

"Ma'am, have you checked with your own clergy?"

"They won't help her! I was advised to come to Baxter. In this village, there is a healer." she explained.

Christopher stopped to gather his thoughts. He was not going to do an exorcism on the girl. But maybe the girl needed some medicine the doctors would not be able to provide. Willow would know what to do for the girl.

"Bring the girl. I will not do an exorcism, but I will try to help. Bring her in an hour," Christopher finally gave into the woman's pleading.

"Thank you! Thank you!" the woman cried.

"Don't thank me until I see the girl and decide whether I can help her. I don't mean to be rude, but I need to prepare for our meeting."

"Of course. I'll be going. See you soon, Pastor," the woman said and left.

Christopher saw a familiar figure walking up his walk. Willow stopped for a couple of minutes to speak to the woman before the woman drove off in her wagon.

"Interesting company," Willow stated.

"That is one word to describe it," Christopher commented.

"You look troubled."

"I am."

"Why? What is troubling you. Must be something great for I can see it in your eyes," Willow observed.

"She wants me to look at her daughter. She said her local clergy won't help her. She wanted me to sprinkle Holy Water on her daughter."

"Did the mother say she was possessed?"

"She said Satan was trying to invade the daughter's mind," he said sighing.

"Did she say how?"

"No. I wanted to talk to you, so I told her to come back in an hour. Did you see the girl?"

"Yes, I saw her and spoke with the mother." Willow shook her head.

"What are your initial thoughts?"

"The truth is not being fully told."

"Meaning?" Christopher asked with concern developing.

"Meaning, someone is being deceived."

"Do you think there is nothing wrong with the girl?"

"I do not think it is the girl that needs protection in the way that you are being led to believe. It is the mother. Her energy did not set right with me. Something just isn't right. I have a plan."

"What do I need to do?" he asked.

"Pray, dear Christopher. Pray harder than you ever have prayed for in your life," Willow said before kissing him on the cheek and walking away.

"Where are you going?" he asked calling after her.

"Don't worry, I'll be back." Willow left him with her smile.

The smile was the last thing he saw as she walked away. But he touched his cheek where she kissed him and grinned sheepishly.

Christopher smiled and laughed to himself as he watched Willow leave. He believed she would be going to her house to gather the items she would need to help the girl and her mother. As soon as she was out of sight, he began to prepare things himself, and of course, pray as he was instructed to do by Willow.

CHAPTER 18

Willow's mind was on the short peck she gave Christopher on the cheek. She was not sure why she kissed him, but it felt right and natural. She smiled when she thought of his green eyes twinkling when he smiled as she was walking away. He made her smile. He made her truly happy.

Her thoughts of Christopher had to be put out of her mind for the time being. Willow needed to concentrate on the task on hand. She knew there was no room for distractions. She quickly gathered the necessities required and rushed back to the church.

"Protect us, dear ones," she said to the gargoyles and patted their limestone heads.

The feeling of caution overwhelmed Willow's body. Something was telling her danger was on the horizon. She couldn't pinpoint it, but something huge was coming. She hoped Christopher's prayers would be heard but more importantly answered.

"Hello," Christopher greeted her.

"Hello," she said with a smile.

"I've been praying."

"I have been preparing."

"What have you been preparing for exactly?" Christopher asked with curiosity.

"What have you been praying for exactly?" she flirted.

"Wisdom in a word." Christopher said with a little bit of grimness in his voice.

"One never reaches full capacity in wisdom. You and I both know only one person has all the wisdom. We can only harvest what He gives us."

"Well, He sure gave you some wisdom. I have an unsettled feeling about this woman."

"You don't have to help her, Christopher. You can walk away. Go with your instinct."

"I will help her. I have you and God on my side," he said with a coy smile.

"Hello?" a frail voice said.

"Hello. Who is there?" Christopher asked the visitor.

"My name is Mari. My mother came to see you earlier. May I come forward to speak to you?" a girl about the age of sixteen came forward.

She was an average height, about five foot five inches. Her strawberry blond hair was flowing loosely about her shoulders. Her skin was golden from the summer sun. She was thin. But there was a deep sadness in her eyes. Willow noticed that immediately.

"Hello, Mari. My name is Pastor Davis. This is my good friend, Willow. Where is your mother? You are here early."

"Please beg the intrusion. My mother is misguided. She is convinced Satan is trying to invade my mind and take my soul. You are the fifth pastor she has contacted in two weeks. I assure you, Pastor, I am not being attacked by Satan. I am as clear minded as a Sunday morning."

"Why would your mother spread such a lie?" Christopher asked.

"Because Satan is attacking her. He wants the focus to be on me so he can invade her. She has been chanting terrible things. She has killed innocent animals and she has this look in her eyes that is indescribable." Mari breathlessly explained.

Willow and Christopher exchanged looks of worry and concern. They both looked at the girl with surprise and doubt. Willow looked at the girl and she could see the girl was frightened. Mari was scared and worried for her safety and the safety of her mother. Christopher had read about demon possession, but he had never seen one in person. Nor did he ever think such a thing could or would happen in Baxter.

"I want you to go and hide. You do not need to be anywhere near your mother right now. The Pastor and I need to have a conversation. Go and don't ever come back to this town again," Willow instructed the girl as she took the frightened girl's hands into her own.

"But what about my mother? How can I leave her?"

"My child, if you don't do as Willow said, you will die. She will kill you. You are not safe here," Christopher informed the girl.

"I don't understand. Isn't a church hallowed ground?"

"It is."

"Pardon my ignorance, Pastor, but why can't I hide in the church?"

"My dear girl, it is not safe. Please listen to my words and go far away from here."

The girl looked at both before speaking, "I will pray for both of you. Please don't hurt her. She was not always as you see her as now. She changed when father died," she said before she took off towards the forest, only looking back once.

"You need to go too," Christopher said to Willow as he watched Mari disappear into the woods.

"I am not going anywhere," Willow firmly stated.

"Willow, this is not your fight."

"How is it yours? Just because you are a man of God?"

Christopher did not know what to say to her. He could see in her eyes he was not going to win the battle with her. He shrugged his shoulders and decided to say nothing more to her. He was not sure what battle they were going to have, but he didn't want to lose two in one day.

"Pastor, I'm sorry my daughter seems to be missing. She ran away," the woman said as she entered the church.

Willow and Christopher exchanged looks.   If Satan were attacking the woman, how could she enter the church? The woman walked in at a steady pace. She looked like a mother who was worried about her daughter.

"You look worried as a mother should be. Here, please have a glass of water." Willow handed her a glass. The woman drank the liquid quickly and asked for more. She drank that glass quickly also. She placed the glass down on the pew and hiccupped.

"Where do you think your daughter has gone?" Christopher asked.

"I am not sure and I'm afraid I wasted your time. When I see my daughter, she shall feel the sting of a tree branch or horse whip for making me look such a fool," she said with anger mounting up from her.

"You will do no such thing! You will not put one finger on that girl," Christopher said with conviction, surprising Willow and himself.

"Do you think you are better than me because you are a man of God?" the woman asked, becoming angrier.

"I'm no better than any other man," Christopher said still holding firm.

"Did you pray, Pastor, before I came? Did you pray for protection? Grace? Forgiveness?" she asked, almost hissing as she walked towards him.

Willow stood there silent, just observing this woman who at first seemed like a desperate mother. The lady in front of them now was quite a different person. This woman was full of evil intent. She was there to do one thing. And that was to do harm.

Willow knew the circumstances were going to change quickly. The woman turned to look at Willow. The look was almost a signal of war. But there was no chance of a flag being raised, at least a white one. A blood-stained flag was a totally different story.

Willow's eyes stayed focused on the woman. She noticed a small change in the woman's facial expression. Her slightly wrinkled face was gradually changing to the skin of a younger woman. The long gray locks were transforming to tight curls. Her fingernails were growing at a rapid rate. Her eyes turned the blackest black Willow had ever seen, even on the darkest, moonless night.

"You need to leave," Christopher said to Willow.

"Awe, look at that, the good and noble minister protecting one of his sheep. Isn't that so Christian-like," the lady mocked.

"I'm not going anywhere," Willow said, standing firm.

"She's right. No one is going anywhere," the woman said, smirking as the church doors slammed shut with such force that it made the windows rattle.

"Who are you?" Christopher demanded.

"I'm the bearer of truth."

"The bearer of truth of what?"

"Of how much of a liar your God is."

"God doesn't lie!" Christopher bellowed.

"My God doesn't lie, but yours is a different story," she said as she pointed a long finger with a long nail at the picture of Jesus.

"Your God?" Christopher asked.

"Come on. You are a smart man. Let me tell you about my God," she answered, smiling at him with a crooked smile.

"I can't wait to hear."

"Take a seat. This will take a while," she said, as the chair from the altar came sliding to behind him, buckling his knees, making his body to fall into it, causing him to wince a bit in pain.

Willow ran to his side. Pastor tried to rise from the chair, only to find he was affixed to the chair. He could wiggle his fingers a bit and move his head, but his body was not getting out of the chair.

"You need to go!" Christopher pleaded with her.

"I told you, I am not going anywhere," she said to him.

"I looked around this building and I am disappointed. There are no pictures of my God. You would think a person who is feared so much would at least be pictured," she said, shaking her head.

"My God is all powerful," Christopher interjected.

"This conversation is boring me. I hate to be bored," she said yawning, mockingly.

She slowly walked up to Christopher with a smile of mischief and traced his outline of his face with her finger. Her sharp fingernail stopped at the tip of his chin. She took her fingernail and flicked his chin like she was sending a bug into orbit. The motion caused him to bleed.

The crimson blood started to flow in a steady stream, dripping onto his white shirt. She took her finger and let a few drops fall on her fingertips, her long nail creating a well for the dripping blood. She slowly raised her finger to her lips and tasted Christopher's blood. She savored the red liquid like it was the first and only drop of liquid in the desert. She didn't speak. She kept smacking her lips to keep the flavor fresh on her tongue.

"I must say, I'm sorely disappointed. I thought a holy man's blood would taste differently."

"What do you want?" Christopher demanded, trying to move in the chair.

"The answer will come in time. Here, drink. Have you ever wondered what your own blood tasted like?" She put her blood-soaked finger on his lips.

Christopher pursed his lips tightly closed. He was not going to let the blood enter his mouth. He struggled to free himself from the invisible hold the chair had on him but without success. She took the bloodless hand to hold the top of his head to keep it from moving.   Her small hand had the strength of one hundred men.

Christopher felt if he would move his head his neck would snap like a branch from her immense strength. His lips were extremely dry, even cracked. The liquid would have eased the pain of chapped lips. But he knew he couldn't allow any blood to enter his mouth. He spit out the blood as the woman tried to put it into his mouth. It hit the woman in her face. She wiped the spit off her face and her eyes became blacker as her anger grew.

Willow made her way behind Christopher, putting her hands on his shoulders to give him some comfort and support.

"Tell me something," the woman questioned. "Do you believe you are going to Heaven? Do you believe you are going to hear the horrible sound of the angels singing, see long lost loved ones, and see those pearly gates?"

"I do, yes," Christopher answered emphatically.

"Do you believe you will be forgiven of all your wrong doings? Everything you have ever done wrong in your life? Every lie? Every indecent thought?" she asked as she glanced up at Willow with a smile.

"The Lord and Jesus Christ are forgiving. All I have to do is ask and I will be forgiven," Christopher testified, his head still in her hand. Willow could see the vein on the side of his head pulsing. Christopher was nervous and angry. He was fighting a battle not only for God, but also his life. He was not going to let this woman know he was scared. If he showed any signs of being weak or scared, he was just as useful as the pigs Jesus ran off the cliff.

The woman released her tight grip on his head. She turned her back on the two and let out the loudest growl Willow had ever heard in her entire life. The growl came from deep within her body. If that is where it originated from, it may have ascended from the depths of Hell. She rushed up to him like a spider rushes the prey she caught in her web. She took the same fingernail, still dripping in blood and burned an upside down cross on his forehead, right between the eyes. The smell of burnt flesh filled the church. Christopher yelled in pain. The echoes of his pain broke Willow's heart and hurt her ears.

The chair started to shake violently. Willow backed away from the chair. The whole altar was shaking as if the earth were going to open up and swallow everything whole. The chair shot up into the air to the ceiling of the church. The chair started to spin as if it were a hurricane. Christopher's body was still glued in the chair, preventing him from flying off. Centrifugal force was still pulling his head to the side with each spin.

"Nolite Daemon!" A voice boomed from the dark back of the church.

The woman turned around quickly to see who was interrupting her. The silhouette of a person could be made out with the small amount of light the church held. The person walked slowly but with a quiet determination. The woman was taken aback when the intruder came to full view.

"Watch it, girl! I'll skin you alive!"

"You can't hurt us! You are a coward!" the girl challenged.

"Silence!"

"You claim you are powerful? You are hiding in a woman. Show yourself, your true self. You say you are all powerful. Your God will help you. If your God is so great. Why does he need his minions to enter another's body? Only cowards hide behind someone or something else," the girl questioned.

"I don't know what you are talking about. See, she is out of her head. Satan must be playing his games and tricks. He is a master deceiver." The woman said as she turned to Willow.

"Satan does not have a hold on me."

"I am your mother! Show some respect."

"You are not my mother."

Willow watched the mother and daughter battle with their words. She was surprised, worried, and relieved the girl came back to the church. The two women were not backing down from one another. The daughter was angry. There was a fire in her eyes which spoke of loss and contempt. The mother was not backing down. The mother and daughter were walking in a circle as if they were observing their prey. The mother wanted the daughter's soul. Maybe the demon wanted a younger, more suitable body for deception. The daughter wanted the demon out of her mother.

Willow could hear whispering in her ears as she watched the show down.

"End it now. End it now."

Christopher was still in the air in the wooden chair. It stopped spinning giving Willow a clear view of his well-being. His chin was still dripping drops of blood onto the floor. The burn on his forehead was scabbing over. The smell was gone, giving relief to Willow's stomach and nose. The burn and pain looked savage on his white forehead.

Willow knew what she had to do. While the girl had the woman distracted, Willow looked up at Christopher, who was barely conscious, gave him a smile, walked to the pulpit and started to whisper.

"Pater Noster
Qui es Caelis,
Sanctificetur Nomen Tuum
Adveniant Regnum Tuum
Fiat Voluntas Tia,
Sicut in caelo et in terra
Panem nostrum cotidignum
Da nobis hodie;
Et dimitte nobsdebita nostra,
Sicut et nos dimittimus
Debitoribus nostris,
Et ne nos inducas in tentationem
Sed libera noa a malo
Amen."

Christopher heard Willow's whispered words and nodded to her to start again. She began again and he joined her.

"Our Father who art in Heaven,
Hallowed be Thy Name
Thy kingdom come thy will be done on earth as it is in Heaven.
Give us this day our daily bread.
Forgive us our trespasses as we forgive those who trespass against us.
Lead us not into temptation but deliver us from evil.
For thine is the kingdom, and the power, and glory forever and ever.
Amen." The two finished together.

Christopher's chair came crashing down from the ceiling. He was immediately released from any unseen forces keeping him in the chair. The woman turned around as if she was seeing Jesus himself standing before her. Willow could feel the anger and contempt radiating from the woman.

"Comnus dulcus," Willow said to Christopher with her palm facing him. He fell into a deep sleep.

"You don't know who you are dealing with, girl," the woman hissed. *"Two bodies you overtook to disguise the way you look*

*Free them now where we dwell and return them straight to Hell
Demons, you have no place, remove you from this time and space
Angels and good can dwell, I command you to go back to Hell.
DAEMONIUN ABLIT!"* Willow's voice echoed in the church.

A big thunderclap sounded as if the church was going to destruct around them. There was a light flashing so bright that Willow was afraid if she looked directly at it, she would surely go blind. The shaking of the building caused debris to fall from the ceiling. She covered Christopher with her body to shield him from any debris falling from the ceiling. Instantly, the light was gone. The shaking of the building lasted for what seemed to be hours but was only a few moments. When she felt it was safe, she raised herself up and surveyed the church.   All was as it was before the woman and her daughter arrived. She looked up at the ceiling and it was perfect with no signs of trauma. She was thankful.

She looked at Christopher's still body lying on the church altar. She could see his chest moving up and down with every deep sleep breath he made. She smiled knowing he was alright. With him lying there on the church altar totally unaware of the thoughts going through her mind, Willow didn't realize how handsome he was. She bent down to brush the hair from his eyes and noticed the burn on his forehead was gone; however, the scratch under his chin remained and started to scab over. She was thankful the injury would be easy to explain.

Christopher started to stir awake from his induced slumber. When he opened his eyes a ray of sun burst into the church through the windows and the doors opened graciously. The church felt warm and safe as a church always should feel.

"Willow? What happened?" he asked as Willow helped him stand.

"What do you remember?" Willow asked.

"I remember a woman asking for help for her daughter.'

"Anything else?"

"No, not until now. Please tell me what happened."

"They tried to rob the church. They attacked you and locked me into the tower. They had a knife," Willow explained, saving him from the truth.

"Are you okay? Did they hurt you?"

"I am fine. I stopped them. All the church is safe. Are you okay?"

"I'm a little sore. I am thankful you and the church are safe. Why would they do such a thing?"

"Greed I suppose. Let's get out of here. I have something to put on that cut at my house."

Christopher touched his chin and felt a scab forming. His body hurt and he had a bit of a headache. He was glad no one was seriously hurt. He looked at Willow in the sunlight of the church and realized he was truly blessed.

"I am ready to get out of here. I love God's house, but I need some fresh air."

The two joined hands and left the church. They walked to Willow's house to treat the cut he received when he was attacked. The walk was quiet and they both enjoyed nature's chatter of the day. Willow glanced at Christopher and smiled. She loved the feel of his hand in hers. She was an incredibly lucky girl, in more ways than one.

CHAPTER 19

A few days had passed since the "robbery" at the church. Around the village, the news spread about the event like wildfire. There were several versions of the story. None of them were even close to what had really happened. Willow knew she could never tell the true events of the day in the church. She wanted to tell Christopher, but she knew he wouldn't believe her. She valued his friendship too much to take the risk, even with the honest truth.

Willow had thought a lot about the day in the church. How did a demon enter a church? Why did this person target Christopher? She thought about what she would do if she had lost Christopher. That thought scared her. She replaced those thoughts with more positive ones.

The scratch on Christopher's chin healed nicely with only a little scar remained. Willow was glad Christopher's memory was not allowing the release of how he received that scar. Christopher prayed and asked God for the ability to forgive his attacker. He prayed for God's grace upon the women who robbed him and caused physical harm to him. He thanked God for keeping the church, himself, and Willow safe.

Christopher was quite bothered by the impact the attempted robbery and the attack would have on the town, the congregation, Willow, and himself. A church needed to be a safe place, a happy place, a place of peace every day of the year of their lives. Willow wanted Christopher to feel all those things again. She knew he would never say a word to anyone. And Christopher's memory was locked.

After much whispering, Sunday finally came. Christopher knew his congregation would want answers and comforting words from him. Feelings were just calming down from the whole fireball incident. Would some think this was the omen that Willow mentioned to Mary? Would the people turn against Willow? Would they turn against him? He was feeling anxious. He kept saying the mantra 'faith over fear' since mid-Saturday. He knew God was on his side. He knew God and his angels had been protecting them that day.

Willow's face was the first he saw when he stepped behind the pulpit. She was in the front pew, waiting for him with a smile. She gazed around the church which was filled with brilliant sunshine. She could hear the birds through the open doors and windows. The church became quiet as soon as he stepped behind the altar. The look of confusion was on his face then quickly was overcome by peace.

He had everyone's attention, even the birds quit singing. He looked out at the congregation's faces trying to determine what they were thinking. His knees started to shake behind the pulpit. He could feel little beads of perspiration start to form on his forehead and his heart was starting to race. He looked down at Willow. She smiled at him and he instantly became more confident. His knees calmed themselves. He took a drink of water, cleared his throat, and began.

"Friends, welcome to this beautiful Sunday morning," he greeted.

"Good morning!" the congregation replied.

"It is no secret what happened a few days ago. I was attacked by two women who wanted money. I was knocked unconscious but thank the Lord I only have a small physical scar under my chin. I know the thought of the ladies still out there is not very comforting to you all. Like many of you, I have asked why this has happened. Why did this happen here? Why did this happen to me? Honestly, I don't want to know why. I was all ready to give a long sermon today. But when I came up to the pulpit, the Bible was opened to The Lord's Prayer. Forgive us our trespasses as we forgive those who trespass against us. Forgiveness is a powerful gift the Lord has given us as believers. Let's recite the Lord's Prayer together."

The congregation recited the Lord's Prayer, sang a few hymns and dispersed for a continued day of celebrating God, friends, and family.

Willow and Christopher were talking to parishioners when they heard familiar footsteps. Those church members quickly dispersed so the person could talk to the two of them.

"Great sermon today, Pastor."

"Thank you."

"Willow. It must have been terrible to be locked up in the tower while Pastor was attacked. I hope you are alright."

"I am fine, thank you."

"I better be going. I just wanted to say hello and see how you were doing," he said before he turned to go.

"Excuse me, Pastor. This must have fallen off a woman's neck," a child said as he brought the Pastor a necklace.

Willow made an inward, silent gasp. She knew the necklace! She remembered the necklace! She moved closer to Christopher to get a closer look at the piece of jewelry.

"Thank you," Christopher said to the child.

"You are welcome," he said and pranced off to join his family.

"What a unique piece of jewelry," Christopher commented as he hung the piece on his finger.

"May I see it?" Willow asked.

Christopher handed the piece to her. It was a unique piece. The energy of the piece was all too familiar. The piece was heavy. How could anyone wear such a thing around the neck? She turned the piece over and found something truly life changing. A.W. engraved on the back of the piece. She looked and there stood Amos Wells in the doorway and a figure beside him. She looked down again at the engraved letters on the piece again and she looked at the doorway again. Amos was gone. Only his laughter remained with the words *"Hoc est super"* echoing in her ears.

EPILOGUE

The words of Amos Wells were repeating in her head like a child begging his mother for a piece of candy. The echoes of the words were beginning to make her temples ache. She raised her fingers to massage the pain.

"Willow, are you alright? You looked pale," Christopher questioned with genuine concern as he touched her elbow as to steady her stance.

"I forgot to eat this morning. My body is telling me I need nourishment and rest. I will be fine when I get to my bed to lie down," she gave her concerned friend a smile.

"Do you want me to fetch my carriage to take you home?"

"The fresh air will do my body good. It is a beautiful day and there will not be many of those left. I need to take advantage while I can but thank you."

"At least come to the house and pick a couple of apples to eat on your way back," he said as he took her hand and led her to his apple trees, not waiting for her to protest.

Willow allowed him to lead her to the beautiful apple grove. All types of apples were growing on the trees. The fruit seemed to be perfect, not a rotten one in the whole bunch. The Good Lord blessed him with a great crop of apples and blessed the animals with a few that had fallen for their nourishment too.

"The Lord is good. The apples are the sweetest you will ever taste. Looking at them so ripe and colorful I can see why the serpent chose an apple tree to tempt Eve. Take a basket full to make a pie."

"Christopher, those are yours. You can make a pie."

"Willow, you take them and you can teach me to make a pie," he smiled and handed her a basket that was on the ground by the tree. The pair picked the apples and shared in light conversation. Quickly the basket was full of shiny, ripe apples that would be perfect for pie baking.

"Thank you for the apples. They will make a great pie. I look forward to showing you how to make one soon."

"You are welcome for the apples and, yes, I look forward to the instruction. You still look pale. Are you sure you don't want me to take you home? It is not a bother at all. It would be my pleasure," Christopher offered again.

"Thank you again for the offer. I appreciate your concern. I will be fine walking. I will go home and rest straight away."

"I will not argue with you for I know I will not win. I will come by tomorrow. Blessed travels home," he said before kissing her on the cheek.

"You have a blessed day also," she said with a smile and turned to walk home.

Willow started her walk to her home. The thought of being in her own home was very comforting to her. The image of Amos in the doorway kept popping up in her mind to remind her of his words.

The weather was perfect. The sun was not too hot but giving enough warmth to keep you warm with just a shawl. It was cool enough for the animals to start gathering food stores for a long winter. The sap of the trees was good at making this prediction. Willow remembered hearing if the sap was thick, winter was on its way soon.

The meadow was preparing for the colder weather also. The sun was gracious enough to shine its warmth so the flowers and plant may flourish as long as they could before the snow took them into a slumber until the vibrant spring. Change was coming. Change was all around. Change could be scary, exciting, and stressful. But change must be embraced. Change was the path to the future and closure to the past. Willow felt extreme comfort when her two stone friends came into her sight. She loved those statues. She knew many would consider her odd to have such fondness for the stone statues. Many even would call them hideous, scary, and odd. What their ignorance showed was that the statues were not scary. The gargoyles were stone angels, her protectors.

Her gaze went to the house. There was smoke coming from the chimney. She knew she didn't leave a fire burning in the fireplace before leaving for church. Her steps quickened to reach her house. Who was in her house? Amos? She finally reached her door, breathless from sprinting. She slowly turned her knob and opened the door. She entered the house with caution. When the door opened, she could feel the warmth of the fire and smell some food cooking.

There standing by the fireplace, she saw an image of herself as an older woman.   The shock made her drop the basket of apples.

"Hello, dear. I have been waiting for you. Come sit down and have some tea. I have a lot to tell you. My name is Scarlett," the woman said as she came forward to embrace Willow.

"Hello, Willow. Welcome to your awakening." Liam Harper said with a welcoming smile.

Dear Friends,

This is Willow Oakes. I know you have several questions. What happened to Adam? What happened to Joseph? The women who attacked us at the church. And many other questions. I promise you that all will be answered in the next book.

I didn't draft this story. The author did an excellent job, but no one can tell the continuation of my story better than myself. I promise your questions will be answered in the next book. You will not have to wait long to discover those answers.

Stay safe until we meet again!

Blessings,

Willow Oakes